UNCOVERING HER NINE MONTH SECRET

UNCOVERING HER NINE MONTH SECRET

BY

JENNIE LUCAS

First published in Great Britain 2014
by Mills & Boon, an imprint of Harlequin (UK) Limited,
Large Print edition 2014
Eton House, 18-24 Paradise Road,
Richmond, Surrey, TW9 1SR

© 2014 Jennie Lucas

ISBN: 978-0-263-24126-6

Printed and bound in Great Britain
by CPI Antony Rowe, Chippenham, Wiltshire

To Pete

PROLOGUE

HE SEDUCED ME EASILY. He broke down my defenses as if they were paper. You wouldn't have been able to resist, either, believe me.

After so many years of feeling like a ghost in my own home, invisible, unloved, I think I would have fallen into his arms for one dark glance—one husky word. But Alejandro gave me so much more than that. He looked at me as if I were the most beautiful woman on earth. Listened to me as if every word on my lips was poetry. He pulled me into his arms, made me burst into flame, kissed my grief and cares away. After so many years of living in a cold gray world, my life exploded into color—because of him.

There was no reason why the Duque de Alzacar, one of the richest men in Spain, would want someone like me—plain, poor—rather than my beautiful, wealthy cousin. I thought it was a miracle.

It was only later that I realized why Alejandro had chosen me. He hadn't seduced me out of love—or even lust. It was many months before I realized the selfish reason that had caused him to overwhelm me with his charm, to dazzle me, to make me love him.

But by then, it was too late.

CHAPTER ONE

THE GRAY, LOWERING sky was falling like a shroud across the old colonial city of San Miguel de Allende when I heard the words I'd feared in nightmares for the past year.

"A man was here looking for you, Señora Lena."

Looking up at my neighbor, I staggered back, clutching my five-month-old son in my arms. "What?"

The woman smiled, reaching out to chuck the cooing baby's pudgy chin. "*Gracias* for letting me watch Miguelito for an hour. Such a pleasure…"

"But the man?" I croaked, my mouth dry. "What did he look like?"

"*Muy guapo,*" she sighed. "So handsome. Dark-haired and tall."

It could be anyone, I told myself desperately. The old silver mining town in central Mexico was filled with American expatriates who'd moved here to enjoy the lovely architecture and take classes at the famous Instituto. Many single women had come here to start new lives, pursuing new businesses as artists and sculptors and jewelry makers.

Like me. A year ago, I'd arrived pregnant and full of grief, but I'd still managed to start a wonderful new life. Perhaps this dark stranger was looking for a portrait of his sweetheart, nothing more.

But I didn't believe it. Fear was cold inside me. "Did he give his name?"

Dolores shook her head. "The baby was fussing in my arms when I answered the door. But the man was well dressed, with a Rolls-Royce. A chauffeur. Bodyguards, even." Her smile spread to a grin. "Do you have a rich new boyfriend, Lena?"

My knees went weak.

"No," I whispered.

It could be only one man. Alejandro Guillermo Valentín Navaro y Albra, the powerful Duke of Alzacar. The man I'd once loved with all my innocent heart. The man who'd seduced and betrayed me.

No. It was worse than that.

"He's not your boyfriend, eh?" My neighbor's voice was regretful. "Pity. Such a handsome man.

Why did he come looking for you, then? Do you know him?"

Beads of sweat broke out on my forehead. "When was he here?"

She shrugged, looking bemused. "A half hour ago. Maybe more."

"Did you say anything about—about Miguel being my son?"

Dolores shook her head. "He didn't give me the chance. He just asked if you lived in the house two doors down. I said yes. He pulled out his wallet and asked me not to mention his visit, because he wanted to surprise you. Can you imagine?" She flourished some bills from her apron pocket in delight. "He paid me a thousand pesos for my silence!"

Yes. I could imagine. I briefly closed my eyes. "But you told me anyway," I whispered. "Bless you."

She snorted. "Men always want to arrive with a flourish of trumpets. I thought it better for you to be prepared." She looked at my shapeless white sundress and plain sandals with a moue of disapproval, then at my long, casual ponytail and makeup-free face. She sighed. "You have a good figure, but in that dress you look like a marshmallow. You don't make the most of yourself. It's almost like you don't *want* to be noticed!" She shook her head. "But tonight you must be at your most irresistible, your most sexy, *sí?* You want him to want you!"

No. I really didn't. Not that he would want me anyway, now his evil plan had succeeded. "He's not my boyfriend."

"So picky!" She made a *tsk* sound. "You don't want *this* billionaire, you don't want *that* one—I tell you, wealthy, handsome men are not so thick upon the ground as you seem to think!" Dolores glared at me. "Your son needs a father. *You* need a husband. Both of you deserve every happiness." Her expression turned suddenly sly. "And the man at my door looked like he would bring a *lot* of happiness to a wife. Every night."

"No doubt," I said over the razor blade in my throat. It was true. Alejandro had brought me intense joy for one summer. And a lifetime's worth of anguish since. "I should go."

"*Sí.* It's almost Miguel's nap time, isn't it, *pequeño?*" she crooned.

My baby yawned, his fat cheeks vying with his sleepy dark eyes for cuteness. Those eyes just like his father's.

I exhaled, running a hand over my forehead. I'd allowed myself to think we were safe. That Alejandro had given up looking for me. *I should have known.* I should have known better than to start sleeping at night, to start making friends, to start making a real home for myself and my son. *I should have known they would someday find me....*

"Lena?" My neighbor frowned. "Is something wrong? You do not seem happy."

"Did you tell him when I'd be back?"

"I wasn't sure when you'd be done, so to be safe I said four o'clock."

I glanced at the clock in her brightly painted front room. It was only three. I had one hour. "Thank you." In a burst of emotion, I hugged her, knowing that she'd been kind to me—to both of us—but I would never see her again after today. "*Gracias,* Dolores."

She patted my back. "I know you've had a hard year, but that's in the past. Your life is about to change for the better. I can always feel these things."

Better? I choked back a laugh, then turned away before she could see my face. *"Adios...."*

"He'll be your boyfriend, just wait and see," she

called after me gleefully. "He'll be your husband someday!"

My *husband*. A bitter thought. I wasn't the one Alejandro had wished to marry. He wanted my wealthy, beautiful cousin, Claudie. It was the whole reason he'd seduced me, the poor relation living in the shadows of Claudie's London mansion. If he and Claudie wed, together they'd have everything: a dukedom, half of Andalucía, political connections across the world, billions in the bank. They'd have almost limitless power.

There was just one thing they could never have.

My eyes fell on my baby's dark, downy head. I clutched Miguel tightly against me, and he gave an indignant cry. Loosening my grip, I smoothed back his soft hair.

"Sorry, I'm so sorry," I choked out, and I didn't know whether I was begging my son's forgiveness for holding him too tightly, for tearing him away from his home or for choosing his father so poorly.

How could I have been so stupid? How?

Hurrying down the small street, I glanced up at the heavy gray sky. August was the rainy season, and a downpour was threatening. Cuddling Miguel against my hip, I punched in the security-alarm code and pushed open the heavy oak door of my brightly painted home.

The rooms inside were dark. I'd fallen in love with this old colonial house, with its tall ceilings, its privacy, its scarcity of windows on the street. I could not have afforded the rent in a million years, but I'd been helped by a friend who'd allowed me to live here rent-free. Well—I thought of Edward St. Cyr as a friend. Until a week ago, when he'd—

But no. I wouldn't think of that now, or how betrayed I'd felt when the friendship I'd come to rely upon had been revealed for what it was.

I'm tired of waiting for you to forget that Spanish bastard. It's time for you to belong to me.

I shuddered at the memory. My answer had sent Edward scowling from this house, back on his private jet to London. There was no way I could remain in this house, living rent-free, after that, so for the past week, I'd looked for a cheaper place to live. But it was hard to find any place cheap enough for the income of a new, self-employed artist. Even here.

San Miguel de Allende had become my home. I would miss the city's cobblestoned streets, growing flowers in my garden and selling portraits in the open-air *mercados*. I'd miss the friends I'd made, Mexicans and expats who'd welcomed an unmarried, heartbroken woman and her baby, who'd taped me up and put me back together.

Now I took a deep breath, trying to steady my shaking nerves. "I can do this," I whispered aloud, trying to make myself believe it. I knew how to grab passports, money and clothes and be out of here in five minutes. I'd done it before, in Tokyo, Berlin, Istanbul, São Paulo and Mumbai.

But then, I'd had Edward to help me. Now I had no one.

Don't think about it, I ordered myself, wiping my eyes. I'd go on foot and hail a taxi on the street. Once at the station, my baby and I would take the next bus to Mexico City. I'd use the emergency credit card Edward had left and fly to the United States, where I was born. I'd head west. Disappear. Once I found a job, I'd pay back Edward every penny.

I'd raise my child in peace, in some small town in Arizona or Alaska, and this time, I'd make sure Alejandro would never, ever find me....

A lamp flicked on in the foyer.

Alejandro was sitting in a chair across the room, staring at me with eyes that burned like fire.

I halted, choking out a gasp.

"Lena Carlisle," he said in a low voice. "At last."

"Alejandro," I breathed as terror racked through me. My hands instinctively tightened on my baby in my arms. "What are you— How did you…"

"How did I find you?" He rose to his feet, tall and broad-shouldered. "Or how did I get in to your house?" His voice was low and husky, with only the slightest accent, blurred from growing up in Spain, followed by years of running a billion-dollar business conglomerate from New York and London. "Do you really think any *security system,* no matter how expensive, could keep me from being where I wanted to be?"

He was even more handsome than I remembered. Seeing him in the flesh, after a year of being tormented by sensual dreams, made my knees tremble. I clutched Miguel closer, willing myself not to faint.

Alejandro's cold eyes never left mine as he walked toward me. He was dressed in black from his well-cut coat to his glossy Italian shoes, draped in *power.*

"What do you want?" I choked out.

He looked from me to my yawning, drowsy-eyed baby.

"Is it true?" His voice was deadly quiet, but the

words burned through my heart. His face was grim. "Is this my baby?"

His baby. Oh, God. Please, no. I stumbled back in blind panic.

"My men are outside. You won't even make it to the street...."

I ignored him. Grabbing the wrought-iron handle, I pulled open the heavy, weathered oak door and started to run. I stopped.

Six hulking bodyguards stood outside my house, in a semicircle, in front of the expensive sedan and black SUV now jamming the slender residential lane.

"Did you think," Alejandro said softly behind me, "that when I finally found you, I would leave anything to chance?"

He stood close behind me, so close I caught the scent of his cologne. So close I could feel the heat emanating from his powerful body. Briefly closing my eyes, I shivered at being so close to the man who had once possessed me, body and soul.

Unwillingly, I turned back to face the ghost who still haunted my heart. His hot black gaze held mine, and in the dark embers of that fire, I was lashed by memories I'd tried so hard to forget. I'd loved him hopelessly from the moment he'd first come to call on my beautiful, wealthy cousin. I'd watched from hallways, made them tea, organized their dinner parties. I'd done it all with a smile, any and all work my cousin required, ignoring the ache of my heart when she bragged after he left that she was going to catch the uncatchable Spanish duke. "He's nearly in my grasp!" Claudie had crowed. "I'll be a duchess before the year is out!"

Then, to everyone's shock, he'd suddenly jilted her.

For me.

He was the first man who'd ever noticed me—really noticed me—and I'd fallen like a stone beneath the sensual onslaught of his power and glamour and dangerous, sexy charm. For six reckless, miraculous weeks in London last summer, Alejandro had held me in his arms, and I felt as if I owned the world.

Memories of the hopes I'd had, the naive girl I'd been, ripped through me now like a torrent of blows. Alejandro's expression was stark, but I could remember his playful smile. The intensity of his dark gaze. The sound of his husky voice whispering sweet words in the night. I could remember hot kisses, and the feel of our naked bodies intertwined in his London hotel suite. In the back of his limo. And once, against the wall in the back stairs of the Carlisle mansion.

Our affair had seemed as infinite as the stars in the sky. But on that bright summer day when I finally gathered the courage to tell him I was in love with him, his smiling face had changed in front of my eyes.

"*Love me?*" Alejandro had repeated scornfully. "You do not even *know* me."

Two minutes later, he was gone, leaving me bereft and bewildered. But the broken, truly broken, came later…

Now, Alejandro took my hand, glancing up and down the quiet Mexican street.

"Come back inside, Lena. We have much to talk about."

Feeling the electricity of his hand wrapped around mine, I looked up with an intake of breath.

He was so close now. Touching me. My lips parted. He was somehow even more devastatingly handsome than I'd remembered. He had the kind of face that could break a woman's heart into a million pieces, to little shimmering fragments of gray dust, leaving you too dazed with his power and beauty to feel anything but gratitude as he lazily destroyed you.

Without my notice, he led me back into the foyer. Reaching over my head, he towered over me, his arm brushing against my hair, his body pressing against mine. I shivered, clutching my baby close. But he merely closed the heavy door with a sonorous bang behind me.

The hard-edged billionaire duke, in his sharply tailored clothes, stood out starkly against my comfortable, bohemian home, with its warm tile floors and walls I'd decorated with homemade paper flowers and my own paintings, one of the Parroquia de San Miguel, but the rest of my baby, the first from when he was just six days old.

Looking down at me, Alejandro said softly, "Is what Claudie told me true? This baby in your arms—it is mine?"

Trembling, I pulled away. Gathering my wits, I glared at him. "Do you really expect me to answer that?"

"It's an easy enough question. There are only two possible answers." Reaching out, he stroked my cheek, but there was no tenderness in his gaze. "Yes. Or no."

"You'd be a horrible father! I won't let my sweet boy be turned into a heartless bastard like—"

"Like me?" His voice was dangerously low. His

dark eyes gleamed in the shadowy foyer. "Is that what you really think of me—after all we once shared?"

Caught in his gaze, I trembled. Once, I might have believed so differently. I'd managed to convince myself that beneath his wealth and power and aristocratic title, Alejandro was decent and good. Like generations of women before me, I had seen what I wanted to see. I'd been blind to the truth, until, against my will, the blindfold had been torn from my eyes.

"Yes. That's what I think of you."

A strange expression flickered across the chiseled planes of his face, an emotion I couldn't identify before it swiftly disappeared. He gave me a sardonic smile.

"You are right, of course. I care for nothing and no one. Least of all you, especially after you and your cousin have gone to such lengths to blackmail me over this child."

"Blackmail you?" I gasped. "You're the one who deliberately seduced me, and got me pregnant, intending to steal my baby away so you could raise him with Claudie!"

He grew very still.

"What are you talking about?" he ground out.

My body was shaking with emotion. "You think I didn't know? When I found out I was pregnant, you'd already left me and gone back to Spain. You wouldn't return my calls. But fool that I was, I was still desperate to share the news, because I hoped you might care! So I begged Claudie for enough money to fly to Madrid. I was scared to tell her why I needed the money. She'd planned so long to marry you. But when I told her I was pregnant, she did something I never imagined."

"What?"

I took a deep breath.

"She laughed," I whispered. "She laughed and laughed. Then she told me to wait. She went into the hallway, but she left the door open and I heard her call you. I heard her congratulate you on your brilliant plan! *Thanking* you, even! How brilliant you were, how clever, to seduce her lowly cousin, the poor relation, to provide the heir you knew she could never give you! Now the two of you could get married immediately." My voice turned acid. "Just as soon as her lawyer forced me to sign papers terminating all my parental rights."

"Yes. She called me." His eyes narrowed. "But I never…"

"'Don't worry, I'll get Lena to sign her baby

away,' she said!" My voice trembled as I remembered the terror I'd felt that day. "She asked you to send over a few security guards from your London office, just in case I tried to fight!" My voice choked and I looked away. "So I ran. Before either of you could lock me away somewhere for the duration of my pregnancy and try to steal my child!"

Silence fell. His eyes narrowed.

"From the day, from the *hour* Claudie told me you were pregnant, I've had investigators trying to track you down, chasing you around the world. Yes, she had some crazy idea that it was her inability to have children that kept me from marrying her. She was wrong." He came closer. "I raced to London, but you were already gone. And ever since, you've always managed to disappear in a puff of smoke whenever I got close. That, *querida,* is expensive. And so is this." He motioned at the high ceilings of the two-hundred-year-old colonial house. "This house is owned by a shell company run out of the Caymans. My investigators checked. So why don't you just admit who's helping you? Admit the truth!"

Something told me not to mention Edward St. Cyr. "And what's that?"

"Once you found out you were pregnant, you knew I would never marry you." His voice softened, his dark eyes almost caressing me. "So you came up with a different plan to cash in, didn't you? You struck a deal…with your cousin."

Whatever I'd expected, it wasn't that. I stared at him. "Are you crazy? Why would Claudie help me? She wants to marry you!"

"I know. After you disappeared, Claudie told me she knew exactly where you were, but that you refused to let me see the child until we could guarantee a stable home. Until I married her."

My lips parted in shock. "But I haven't spoken to Claudie for a year. She has no idea where I am!" I shook my head. "Did she really try to blackmail you into marriage?"

"Women always want to marry me," he said grimly. "They think nothing of stealing or cheating or lying for it."

I snorted. "Your ego is incredible!"

"It's not ego. Every woman wants to be the wife of a billionaire duke. It's not personal."

Of course it is, I thought unwillingly, my heart twisting in my chest. How could any woman not fall in love with Alejandro, and not want him for her own?

"But what I want to know is…" His voice became dangerously low. "Is this baby in your arms truly mine? Or is it just part of some elaborate plot you've set up with Claudie?"

My head snapped back. "Are you asking me if my son is some kind of *stunt baby?*"

"You would be surprised," he said tightly, "how often in life someone pretends to be something they are not."

"You think I'd lie about this—for money?"

"Perhaps not. Perhaps for some other reason." He paused. "If you were not working for Claudie, perhaps you were working for yourself."

"Meaning what?"

"You hoped that playing hard to get, disappearing with my child, would make me want to pin you down. To marry you." He lifted a dark eyebrow. "Not a bad calculation."

My mouth had fallen open. Then I glared at him. "I would never want to be your wife!"

"Right."

His single small word was like a grenade of sarcasm exploding all over me. For an instant my pride made me blind with anger. Then I remembered the dreams I'd once had and my throat went tight. I took a deep, miserable breath.

"Maybe that was what I wanted once," I whispered. "But that was long ago. Before I found out you'd coldheartedly seduced me so you could marry Claudie and steal my baby."

"You must know now that was never true."

"How can I be sure?"

He shook his head. "I never intended to marry Claudie or anyone."

"Yes, you said that. You also told me once that you never intended to have children. And yet here you are, fighting for a DNA test for Miguel!"

"I do not have a choice." His expression changed as he said sharply, "You named the baby Miguel?"

"So?"

"Why?" he demanded, staring at me with a sudden suspicious glitter in his eyes that I did not understand.

"After the beautiful city that took me in—San Miguel became our home!"

He relaxed imperceptibly. "Ah."

Now I was the one to frown. His reaction to our baby's name had been so fierce, almost violent. Had he wondered if I'd named him after another man? "Why do you care so much?"

"I don't," he said coldly.

My baby whimpered in my arms. Fiercely, I

shook my head as I hugged him close, breathing in Miguel's sweet baby scent, feeling his tiny warm body against me. I nuzzled his head and saw tears fall onto his soft dark hair. "If you didn't get me pregnant on purpose, if it happened by accident and you don't want a child…just let us go!"

His jaw tightened. "I have an obligation…."

"Obligation!" I cried. "To you, he's just someone to carry on your title and name. To me, he's everything. I carried him for nine months, felt him kick inside me, heard his first cry when he was born. He's my baby, my precious child, my only reason for living." I was crying openly now, and so was my baby, either in sympathy or in alarm or just because it was past his nap time and all the adults arguing wouldn't let him sleep. Miguel's chubby cheeks were red, his eyes swimming with piteous tears. I tried to comfort him as I wept.

Alejandro's expression was stone. "If he's my son, I will bring both of you to live with me in Spain. Neither of you will ever want for anything, ever again. You will live in my castle."

"I'd never marry you, not for any price!"

"Marriage? Who said anything about that?" His

lips twisted. "Though we both know you'd marry me in a second if I asked."

Stung, I shook my head furiously. "What could you offer me, Alejandro? Money? A castle? A title? I don't need those things!"

He moved closer to me, his eyes dark.

"Don't forget sex," he said softly. "Hot, deep, incredible sex."

In the shadowy hacienda, Alejandro looked at me over the downy head of the baby that we had created. My breasts suddenly felt heavy, my nipples tightening. My body felt taut and liquid at once.

"I know you remember what it was like between us," he said in a low voice. "Just as I do."

I lifted my gaze to his.

"Yes," I whispered. "But what use are any of those things really, Alejandro? Without love, it's empty." I shook my head. "You must know this. Because the money, the palaces, the title—and yes, even the sex… Have those things ever made *you* happy?"

He stared at me. For a long moment, there was only the soft patter of the rain against the roof, our baby's low whimper, and the loud beat of my aching heart.

Then abruptly, for the first time, Alejandro looked, really looked, at our son. Reaching out, he stroked Miguel's soft dark hair gently with a large, powerful hand.

As if by magic, our baby's crying abruptly subsided. Big-eyed, Miguel hiccupped his last tears away as father and son took measure of each other, each with the same frown, the same eyes, the same expression. It would have been enough to make me grin, if my heart hadn't been hurting so much.

Suddenly our baby flopped out a tiny, unsteady hand against Alejandro's nose. Looking down at him in surprise, Alejandro snorted a laugh. He seemed to catch his breath, looking at Miguel with amazement, even wonder.

Then he straightened, giving me a cold glare.

"There will be a DNA test. Immediately."

"You expect me to allow a doctor to prick my baby's skin for a blood test, to prove something I don't want to be proved? Forget it! Either believe he's your son, or—better yet—don't! And leave us in peace!"

Alejandro's face looked cold and ruthless. "Enough."

He must have pressed a button or something—

or else he had some freaky bodyguard alert, like a dog whistle I couldn't hear—because suddenly two bodyguards came in through the front door. Without even looking at me, they kept walking through the foyer, headed across the courtyard toward the bedroom I shared with Miguel.

I whirled on Alejandro. "Where are they going?"

"To pack," he replied coolly.

"Pack for whom?"

A third bodyguard who'd come up silently behind me suddenly lifted Miguel out of my arms.

"No!" I cried. I started for him, arms outstretched, but Alejandro held me back.

"If the DNA test proves he is not my son," he said calmly, "I will bring your son back to you, safe and sound, and I'll never bother either of you again."

"Let me go!" I shrieked, fighting him—uselessly, for with his greater power and strength, his grip was implacable. "You bastard! You bastard! I will *kill* you! You can't take him from me—Miguel! *Miguel!*"

"You are so sure he is mine?"

"Of course he is yours! You know you were my only lover!"

"I know I was your first…."

"My only! *Ever!* Damn you! *Miguel!*"

Something flickered in Alejandro's eyes. But I was no longer looking at him. I was watching as the bodyguard disappeared through the door, my baby wailing in the man's beefy arms. I struggled in Alejandro's grip. "Let me go!"

"Promise to behave, Lena," he said quietly, "and I will."

How I wished I could fight him. If only I had the same power he did—then we'd see who gave orders! If I had his physical strength, I would punch him in the face! If only I had a fortune, a private jet, my own bodyguard army…

My lips parted on an intake of breath.

Edward.

Would he help me? Even now?

That wasn't the question.

Would I be willing to pay the price?

"I don't want to separate you from the baby," Alejandro said, "but I must have the DNA test. And if you're going to fight and scream…"

I abruptly stopped struggling. Nodding, I wiped my eyes. "I'll come quietly. But please," I said softly, looking up at his face, "before you take him to Spain, could we stop in London?"

He frowned. "London?"

I nodded, trying to hide my eagerness—my desperation. "I left something at Claudie's house. Something precious. I need it back."

"What is it?"

"My baby's legacy."

He lifted a dark eyebrow. "Money?"

"And also," I said on a wave of inspiration, "if we could talk to Claudie, together, we could force her to admit how she played us both. Then maybe we could actually trust each other, going forward...."

Alejandro rubbed the back of his head, then nodded. "That would be better. And to be honest, there are a few things I'd like to discuss with your cousin myself."

His voice was grim. I believed him now when he said he didn't want to marry Claudie. Maybe Alejandro hadn't deliberately planned to get me pregnant after all.

But I'd been right about one thing. He still planned to steal my baby. He intended to keep Miguel at his side, to raise him as his heir in some cold Spanish castle, until he turned him into some heartless, unfeeling bastard like himself.

And Alejandro didn't intend to marry me. So I'd be powerless. Expendable.

"So we have a deal?" Alejandro said. "You'll allow the DNA test, and if he is my son, you'll come with us to Spain?"

"With a stop in London first."

"Yes. London. But after that, Spain. I have your word?"

"I honestly hate you," I whispered with feeling.

"I honestly do not care. Do I have your word?"

I glared at him. "Yes."

He looked down at me in the shadows. For a moment, there was a current of electricity between us, sparking in the shadows of the room. His fingers tightened. Then he abruptly released me.

"Thank you," he said coldly, "for being so reasonable."

Hiding the cold determination in my heart, I left him without a word, and nearly sprinted toward my baby.

Alejandro thought he owned me now. But I wasn't as helpless as he thought. I had one card left to play, if I was willing to pay for it.

Was I?

For my son?

Yes. I was.

CHAPTER TWO

THE FIRST TIME I saw London, I was a grief-stricken fourteen-year-old, newly orphaned, just arrived from New York. My grandmother, whom I'd never met, sent her driver to collect me from Heathrow. The sky was weeping and gray. I remembered trembling as I walked up the steps of the tall white mansion in Kensington, a house roughly the same size as my entire apartment building in Brooklyn.

Brought in by the butler, I'd found my grandmother sitting at her antique desk in the morning room. I stood in front of the fireplace for some moments, my eyes stinging and my heart aching, before she finally looked up.

"So you're Lena," she'd said, looking me up and down, from the lumpy coat my mother had made before her hands grew frail in illness, wasting away like her heart since my father's death six months previously, down to my feet crammed into cheap, too-small shoes that had been all my loving but sadly unskilled father had been able to afford. "Not much of a beauty," she'd said crisply, with some regret.

It was raining in London today, too.

As Alejandro's driver waited, holding open my door, I shivered, looking up at the white mansion. I felt suddenly fourteen again. Except now I was going to face my cousin.

Claudie and I were the same age, but she was so different in looks and manner that we could have been born on opposite sides of not just the Atlantic, but the universe.

When I'd first come to the house—devastated by the loss of both my mother and my father within six short months—I'd tried so hard to make my beautiful, spoiled cousin like me, but she'd scorned me on sight. She'd been determined to drive me from the house. Especially once grandmother died and she saw the terms of the will. And she'd finally gotten her wish. She'd won....

"What are you waiting for?" Alejandro said impatiently. "Get out of the car."

"I changed my mind. I don't need to go in."

"Too bad. You're going."

He looked far too handsome and rested. He'd slept and showered on his private jet. He was in a fresh suit. I, on the other hand, hadn't slept at all since yesterday. After an interminable visit to a private hospital in San Miguel de Allende, where he'd paid a small fortune for the DNA test, we'd gotten on his private 747 and I'd spent the long flight walking back and forth in the cabin, trying to calm Miguel enough to sleep. But the cabin pressure hurt his ears, and only my continual walking soothed him. So I'd gotten exercise, at least, using the aisle of Alejandro's jet as my own private treadmill.

But there'd been no shower for me. I felt groggy, sweaty and dirty, and I was still wearing the same white cotton sundress I'd worn in Mexico. There was no way I was going to face my cousin like this.

It was bad enough letting Alejandro see me.

He'd barely said ten words to me on the plane; in fact, he'd said just five: "Want me to hold him?" Of course, I refused. I hadn't wanted to give up possession of my baby, even for a moment. Even thirty thousand feet in the air, when there was no way for him to run off. The DNA test had proved the obvious—that Alejandro was Miguel's father—but I was fighting his emotional and legal claim with every cell and pore.

Now, as Alejandro looked at me in the backseat, the difference between his sleek gorgeousness and my chubby unattractiveness was so extreme I imagined he must be asking himself what he could ever have seen in me. Which begged the question: If he hadn't deliberately seduced me last summer to create an heir, then why on earth had he?

I licked my lips. "Alejandro," I said hesitantly. "I…"

"Enough delay," he growled. "We're going in."

I looked at my baby, tucked into a baby seat beside me in the back of the limo, now sleeping in blessed silence. "You go. I'll stay here with Miguel." Which would also be the perfect way for me to sneak to Edward's house, at the end of the street.

"Dowell can watch him."

I glanced at the driver doubtfully. "No."

"Then bring Miguel with us."

"Wake him up?" I whispered, scandalized. I narrowed my eyes. "Of course *you* wouldn't worry about that. You're not the one who spent the whole flight walking in circles trying to make him sleep."

Alejandro set his jaw. "I offered to take him…."

"You could have offered again." I was dimly aware that I sounded irrational. There was no way he could have taken Miguel from me on the jet except by force, which wouldn't exactly have gone over well, either. My cheeks got hot. "It doesn't matter."

He lifted a dark eyebrow. "You do know how to take care of Miguel better than I do."

His tone told me whom he blamed for that. "I had no choice. I thought you were going to steal him from me."

"So you stole him first?"

I blinked. I hadn't thought of it that way before.

"You could at least have called me directly," he ground out.

Now, that was unfair! "I tried! You wouldn't take my phone calls!"

"If I'd known you were pregnant, I would have." His jaw tightened. "You could have left a message with Mrs. Allen…."

"Leave a *message* with some faceless secretary at your London office to let you know, oh, hey, I'm pregnant with your baby? Seriously?" I lifted my chin. "You should have just taken my damn call!"

Alejandro stared at me, his lips pressed in a thin line. "This argument is over." He turned away.

"Unlatch the baby carrier and lift it out of the seat. That won't wake him up, as you know perfectly well."

My cheeks burned slightly. Yes, I'd known that. I'd just been hoping *he* wouldn't.

When I didn't move, Alejandro started to reach around me. With a huff I turned and unlatched the seat. Miguel continued softly snoring in sweet baby dreams, tucked snugly in the carrier with a soft blanket against his cheek.

As the driver closed the door behind us with a snap, I stood on the sidewalk, staring up at the cold white mansion.

I'd never wanted to return to this house. But there was one silver lining. I hadn't been lying when I'd told Alejandro I wanted to come back for Miguel's legacy. Something I'd been forced to leave behind that had nothing to do with the inheritance I'd lost.

As I looked up, the soft drizzle felt like cobwebs against my skin. Like memories. Like ghosts.

"What now?" Alejandro was glaring at me as if I wasn't his favorite person. I couldn't blame him. He wasn't my favorite person right now, either.

Although at this moment there was one person I liked even less. I swallowed.

"I'm scared," I whispered.

He stared at me. "Of Claudie?"

I nodded, not trusting my voice.

"You don't need to be scared," he said gruffly. "I'm here with you now." Reaching out, he took the baby carrier from my trembling hands. "Come on."

Alejandro carried our sleeping baby up the stone steps and knocked on the imposing front door.

Mr. Corgan, the longtime butler, opened the door. His jowly face was dignified as he greeted Alejandro.

"Good morning, Your Excellency." Then he glanced at me and his eyes went wide. "Miss Lena!" He saw the sleeping baby in the carrier, and the usually unflappable Mr. Corgan's jaw fell open. "It's true?" He breathed, then glanced at Alejandro, and the mask slipped back into place. Holding open the door, he said sonorously, "Won't you both please come in?"

He led us into the elegant front salon, with high ceilings and gilded furniture. Everything looked just as I remembered—vintage, French and expensive. I'd been allowed in this room only a handful of times, the last being when I'd begged Claudie for money to fly to Spain. The day my life had fallen apart.

Mr. Corgan said, "I regret that Miss Carlisle is… out…at the moment, but she has a standing order to welcome you at any time, Your Excellency, if you care to wait."

"*Sí,*" Alejandro said coldly. "We will wait."

"Of course. She will be so pleased to see you when she returns. May I offer refreshments? Tea?"

Alejandro shook his head. He sat down on the pink striped couch near the window. He seemed incongruous there, this dark, masculine Spaniard with severely tailored black clothes, in a salon that looked like a giant powder puff, with the powder made of diamond dust.

He set down the baby carrier on the white polished marble floor beside the sofa. I swiftly scooped it up, and exhaled in relief now that my sleeping baby was safely back in my possession. I followed Mr. Corgan out of the salon and into the hallway.

Once we were alone, the butler's mask dropped and he turned to face me with a happy exclamation.

"We missed you, girl." He hugged me warmly. I closed my eyes, smelling pipe smoke and brass polish. Then I heard a crash and pulled back to see Mrs. Morris, the housekeeper, had just broken a china plate in the hallway. But she left it there, coming forward with a cry.

A minute later, both of them, along with Hildy, the maid, were hugging me and crying and exclaiming over Miguel's beauty, his dark hair, his fat cheeks.

"And such a good sleeper, too," Mrs. Morris said approvingly. Then they all looked at each other. I saw the delicate pause.

Then Hildy blurted out, "Who's his father, then?"

I glanced back at the salon, biting my lip. "Um…"

Hildy's eyes got huge when she saw who was in the salon. Then she turned to Mr. Corgan. "You were right. I owe you a fiver."

His cheeks went faintly pink as he cleared his throat with a *harrumph*. "I might have heard some of your conversation with Miss Carlisle the day you left, Miss Lena." He shook his jowly head with a glare. "It wasn't right what she did. Driving you from the house a year before you would have got your grandmother's inheritance."

I was surprised for only a second. Then I gave a

wry smile. Of course they knew. Household staff knew everything, sometimes even before their employers did. "It doesn't matter."

"But it does," Mrs. Morris said indignantly. "Miss Carlisle wanted your inheritance and the moment she convinced you to move out of the house, she got it by default. Just a year before it would have finally been yours!"

I pressed my hand against my temple as emotions I had spent the past year trying to forget churned up in me.

When I turned eighteen, I could have left for college, or gotten a real job. Instead, I'd remained living in this house, working as a sort of house manager/personal assistant for my cousin beneath her unrelenting criticism as she tried her best to drive me away. I'd had a small salary at first, but even that had disappeared when she'd lazily announced one day that she was cutting the salaries of the staff by twenty percent. "They don't need it," she sniffed. "They are lucky, working all day in my beautiful house. They should be paying *me!*"

Mr. Corgan and Mrs. Morris and the rest had become my friends, and I knew they had families to support. So I'd given up my salary rather than see them suffer. Leaving me virtually destitute for years, in spite of working eighteen-hour days.

But I hadn't minded, not really, because I'd known all I had to do was remain in this house until I was twenty-five, just a few months from now, and I would have gotten the huge inheritance once destined for my father, before he'd been cut out of the will for the crime of marrying my mother.

Eight years ago, when my grandmother lay dying, she'd clutched his old teddy bear and dissolved in tears I'd never seen before as she remembered the youngest son she'd once loved best. She'd called for her lawyer.

If Robert's child proves herself worthy of the Carlisle name, my grandmother's will had read, *and she still lives in the house at the age of twenty-five, she may claim the bequest that would have been his.*

But now it had all reverted to Claudie. I hadn't cared a whit about the money last year, when I'd feared my baby would be stolen from me. But now...

"The house hasn't been the same without you, Miss Lena," Mr. Corgan said.

"Half the staff resigned after you left," Mrs. Morris said.

"She's been intolerable without you to run interference." Mr. Corgan shook his head grimly. "I've worked for this family for forty years, Miss Lena, but even I fear my time here is nearing an end." Leaning closer, he confided, "Miss Carlisle still insists she'll marry your duke."

"He's not my duke...."

"Well. He's the only man rich and handsome enough for *her,* though she says she'd marry any rich idiot who'd make her a duchess...." Glancing back over his shoulder, he coughed, turning red.

Turning, I saw Alejandro standing in the doorway of the salon. I wondered how much he'd heard. His face was half hidden in shadow, his expression inscrutable.

"Did you change your mind about the tea, Your Excellency?" Mr. Corgan gasped, his face beet red.

Alejandro shook his head. His eyes were dark, but his lips quirked at the edges. "We rich idiots prefer coffee."

The butler looked as if he wished the earth would swallow him up whole. "I'll get it right away, sir...."

"Don't bother." He looked at me. "Did you get what you came for?"

He'd heard everything, I realized. He thought I'd come for my inheritance. He thought that was the precious thing that had brought me here. It wasn't.

I turned to Mrs. Morris urgently. "Did she throw out my things?"

"She wanted to," she said darkly. "She told me to burn it all. But I boxed it all up and left it in your attic room. I knew she'd never bother to go all the way up there to check."

"Bless you," I whispered, and hugged her. "Stay and have coffee," I called to Alejandro. "I'll be back in a few minutes." I started up the stairs, carrying my sleeping baby with me.

Climbing three floors, I reached the attic. It looked even more desolate than I remembered, with only one grimy window, an ancient metal bed frame and stacks of boxes. Setting down the baby, I went straight for the boxes.

"What are you looking for?"

Hearing Alejandro's husky voice behind me, I turned. "These boxes hold everything from my childhood."

He stepped inside the attic room, knocking his head against the slanted roof. He rubbed it ruefully. "I can see why Claudie wouldn't come up here. This place is like a prison cell."

"This was my home for over ten years."

His dark eyes widened. "This room?" He slowly looked around the attic, at the rough wood floors, at the naked lightbulb hanging from the ceiling. "You lived here?"

I gave a wistful laugh. "From the time my parents died when I was fourteen, until I left last year when…well. It looked nicer then, though. I made decorations, paper flowers." A lump rose in my throat as I looked around the bare room where I'd spent so many years. The bare mattress on the metal bed frame where I'd slept so many nights. I gently touched the bare lightbulb and swung it on the cord. "I had a bright red lampshade I bought from the charity shop on Church Street."

"A charity shop?" he said sharply. "But you're Claudie's cousin. A poor relation, I know, but I'd assumed you were well paid for all your work…."

This time my laugh was not so wistful. "I was paid a salary after I turned eighteen, but that money had to go to—other things. So I started earning a little money doing portraits at street fairs. But Claudie allowed me so little time away from the house…"

"*Allowed* you?" he said incredulously.

I looked at him. "You heard about my inheritance."

"How much would it have been?"

"If I was still living in this house on my twenty-fifth birthday, a few months from now, I would have inherited thirty million pounds."

His jaw dropped.

"Thirty…"

"Yes."

"And you left it all?"

"To protect my baby. Yes."

"To protect our baby, you sacrificed more money than most people see in a lifetime."

He sounded so amazed. I shook my head. "Any mother would have done the same. Money is just money." I glanced down at Miguel, and a smile lifted my cheeks as I said softly, "He is my life."

When I finally looked up, his dark, soulful eyes were looking at me as if he'd never seen me before. My cheeks went hot. "I expect you think I'm an idiot."

"Far from it," he said in a low voice.

He was looking at me with such intensity. Awkwardly, I turned away and started digging through the top box. Pushing it aside, I opened the one beneath it.

"What are you looking for?" he said curiously.

Not answering, I pulled out old sweaters, old ragtag copies of books I'd read and reread as a teenager, *Rebecca, A Little Princess, Jane Eyre.* Finally, at the bottom of the box, I found the three oversize, flat photo albums. "Thank you," I whispered aloud when I saw they hadn't been burned, or warped from being left to rot in the rain or scribbled on with a venomous black marker, or any of the other images I'd tormented myself with. Pressing the albums against my chest, I closed my eyes in pure gratitude.

"Photo albums?" Alejandro said in disbelief. "You begged me to come to London for *photo albums?*"

"I told you," I said sharply. "I came for my baby's legacy."

"But I never thought..." Frowning, Alejandro held out his hand. "Let me see."

Reluctantly, I handed them over, then watched as he turned through the pages of the top album, at old photographs pressed against yellowing adhesive pages beneath the clear plastic cover.

"It nearly killed me to leave them behind," I

said. "It's all I have left of my parents. My home."
I pointed to a picture of a tenement building where
the ground floor was a butcher's shop. "That was
our apartment in Brooklyn."

He turned the page. "And this?"

My heart twisted when I saw my mother, young
and laughing, holding a ragtag bouquet of flowers,
sitting in my father's lap. "My parents' wedding
day. My dad was a student in London. He fell in
love with a waitress, an immigrant newly arrived
from Puerto Rico. He married her against his family's wishes, when she was pregnant with me…."

Alejandro looked at me for a long moment, then
silently turned more pages. My babyhood flashed
before my eyes, pictures of me as a tiny baby, getting bathed in the sink, sitting on a towel on the
kitchen floor, banging wooden spoons against a
pot and beaming with the same chubby cheeks
that Miguel had now.

Finishing the first album, Alejandro handed it
to me without a word, and thumbed through the
second book, then the third. My childhood passed
swiftly—learning to ride a bike…my first day at
school…

"Why are you interested?" I said haltingly. "Is
it—to make fun of me?"

"To make fun?" He looked at me with a scowl. "You think I would taunt you about having a happy childhood?" He shook his head. "If anything, I envy you," he said softly, looking back at the pages that my tenderhearted mother had made for me when I was a child. Right up to the very last photo, of my father at Christmas, sitting beneath the tree wearing a Santa hat, smiling lovingly at the camera as he held my mother's homemade gift of a sweater. Two months later, he was dead. There were no more photos. The last few pages of the album were blank. Alejandro said softly, "I have no pictures of myself with my mother. None."

I blinked. "How is that possible? I mean, I'd think you'd have a million pictures taken...."

He abruptly looked at me. Without answering, he closed the photo album and handed it to me.

"Perhaps you're not who I thought you were."

"Who did you think I was?"

"Exactly like all the other women I've ever dated. In love with the idea of being a rich duchess." He looked down at me, his dark eyes infinite and deep as the night sky. "But I'm starting to think you're different. A woman who would willingly leave thirty million pounds… You were actually in love with me, weren't you?"

My breath got knocked out of me.

"That was a long time ago."

Our eyes met, and I suddenly had to get out of the attic. I picked up Miguel's baby carrier with one arm and carried the albums with the other. "I'll be downstairs."

Without looking back, I fled, rushing down the flights of stairs. My teeth were chattering, and I was shaking with strange emotion. *Edward,* I reminded myself. The other reason I'd come to London. I had to get his help before Alejandro could bully me into going to Spain. Although it actually wasn't going to Spain that frightened me. It was never being able to leave again. It was being separated from my baby. It was being completely under the control of a man who'd almost destroyed me once, just by making me love him.

As I reached the bottom of the staircase, I heard a car door slam outside. Through the windows, I saw a flash of purple.

Claudie had come home.

I turned to where Hildy was loitering at the bottom of the stairs. "Hildy!"

"Oh, hello," she said, blushing when she saw me. "I was just dusting the banister, Miss—"

"My cousin is here. Please." Grabbing Hildy's arm, I whispered, "I need you to take a message to Edward St. Cyr."

"Edward St. Cyr?" Hildy's eyes nearly popped out of her head. "Mr. St. Cyr himself? Are you serious?"

"Tell him I need to see him," I said with more assurance than I felt.

"Here, miss? You know he and Miss Carlisle hate each other…."

Hearing my cousin fumbling at the door, I shook my head. "Tell him…the Princess Diana Playground in thirty minutes."

With a quick, troubled nod, Hildy hurried toward the back door. Just in time, too. The front door slammed.

"Well. Look who's back."

My cousin's voice was a sneer. Warily, I turned to face her for the first time in a year.

"Hello, Claudie." She was wearing a tight, extremely short bandage dress, the kind you might wear to a club if you wanted a lot of attention, in a vivid shade of purple that almost matched the hollows beneath her eyes. "Late night?" I said mildly.

She glared at me.

"If you came to beg for your inheritance, forget it. My solicitors went through the will with a fine-tooth comb," she ground out. "You'll never…" Then she saw the baby and gasped in triumph. "You brought the brat here? I knew you'd see reason." She rubbed her hands together in glee. "Now I'll either make him marry me, or else I'll—"

"You'll what, Claudie?" Alejandro said coolly from the top of the stairs.

My cousin looked up, speechless for the first time in her life. But she recovered almost instantly. Smiling up at him, she put her hand on her hip, setting a pose that showed her figure to advantage, wearing her six-inch heels and skin-tight purple dress, trailing a cloud of expensive perfume. Her gorgeous, long blond hair tumbled over her shoulders, emphasizing the bone structure of her sharp cheekbones.

But as she licked her big lips, beneath her smile, her eyes were afraid. "Alejandro. I didn't know you were here."

He came down the stairs, looking down at her. He stopped in front of her. Even though she wore such high heels, he was still taller.

"You lied to me, Claudie," he said pleasantly.

"Lena wasn't holding my baby hostage. You were."

She visibly trembled, then tried to laugh. Reaching into her crystal-encrusted bag, she got out a pack of cigarettes. "Darling, I don't know what kind of lies my precious cousin might have told you, but…"

He grabbed her wrist almost violently.

"Do not," he said coldly, "smoke near my son."

"*Your* son," she breathed, searching his gaze, then ripped her arm away. "Are you so sure of that?" Her beautiful blue eyes hardened. "How do you know he's yours? You should have seen all the men who used to come through here, Alejandro—trooping up to Lena's bedroom every single night—"

A little gasp escaped me, like an enraged squeak.

Alejandro lifted an eyebrow. "Then they must have been lost, on their way to *your* room, Claudie."

Her eyes narrowed. "I don't like what you're implying—"

"We did a DNA test," he said, cutting her off. "The baby is mine."

For a moment, she stared at him. But you could

almost see her gather her forces. "He doesn't have to be." She looked from him to me. "If you don't treat him like your son, no one else will."

"You think I would abandon my own child?"

"Fine," she said impatiently. She flung a skeletal finger toward my sweetly sleeping son. "We can take her baby. She's nobody, Alejandro. She won't be able to stop us...."

With a gasp, I protected the baby carrier with my body.

"Just think." Claudie swayed her hips as she walked toward Alejandro with her hypnotic red smile. "Just think how perfect our future could be." She started to wrap her arms around him. "With your money and title, and my money and connections...the two of us could rule the world."

He looked down at her coldly. "Do you really think I'd want to rule the world, if the price would be marriage to you?"

Shocked, she let her arms fall to her sides.

"You used Lena for years as an unpaid slave," he said, "then threatened to take her baby, for the sake of stealing what you wanted—her inheritance. And then you tried to blackmail me into marrying you!"

She licked her lips. "I..."

He held up his hand sharply, cutting her off. His voice was deep and harsh. "For the past year, you've lied to me, saying if I ever wanted to see my child, I had to marry you. Blaming Lena, making me think she was the one to blame. For that, you deserve to go to hell. Which I hope you will find—" he gave her a sudden, pleasant smile "—very soon. *Adios,* Claudie." Scooping up the baby carrier, he turned to me gravely. "Shall we go?" Without another word, he walked out the front door.

"Alejandro, wait," Claudie gasped, but I was the only one left to hear. *"You."* Her face as she turned to look at me really did look like a snake's. Or maybe a dragon's—I could almost see the smoke coming out of her nostrils as her blue, reptilian eyes hardened. "You did this!"

For the past decade, I'd dreamed of what I would say to her if given the chance, after all my lonely years, crying alone in my attic. All the subtle and not so subtle ways she'd insulted me, used me, made me feel worthless and invisible for the past ten years. But in this moment, all those things fled from my mind. Instead, the real question came from my heart.

"Why did you hate me, Claudie?" I whispered,

lifting my tearful gaze to hers. "I loved you. You were my only family. Why couldn't you love me? Why wouldn't you let me love you?"

My cousin drew herself up, all thin gorgeousness.

"Why?" She lit her cigarette with shaking hands. "Because you're not my real family." Taking a long draw on her cigarette, she said in a low, venomous hiss, "And you're not good enough for Alejandro. Blood always tells. Sooner or later, he will be embarrassed by you, just as I was. He'll take your child and toss you in the gutter, like you deserve."

My mouth fell open as her poisoned dart hit me, square in the heart.

"It didn't have to be this way," I choked out, and I turned and fled, still holding my photo albums against my chest, like a shield.

Outside, a sliver of sun had split through the dark clouds, through the rain. Stopping on the sidewalk, I turned back and looked up at the Carlisle mansion for one last time.

"Goodbye," I whispered.

Then I climbed into the limo, where the driver waited with my door open, and he closed it behind me.

"Enjoy a tender farewell?" Alejandro was already in the backseat, on the other side of Miguel, who had woken and was starting to whimper.

"Something like that," I muttered, trying to surreptitiously wipe my tears.

"I was surprised. It's not like you to let me walk off with—" His voice cut off as he saw my face. "What's wrong?"

"Nothing," I said. Turning to my baby, I pressed his favorite blanket against his cheek and tried to comfort him. Tried to comfort myself. My baby's tears quieted and so did his quivering little body, as he felt the hum and vibration of the car's engine beneath him. His eyelids started to grow heavy again.

"What did she say?" Alejandro said. Frowning, he looked closer at my face. "Did she..."

There was a sudden hard knock on his window. Miguel's little body jerked back awake, and his whimpers turned to full-on crying. Alejandro turned with a growl.

Claudie stood by the limo, her eyes like fire. "Open this window!" she yelled through the glass.

Alejandro's expression was like ice as he rolled it down a grudging two inches. She leaned forward, her face raw with emotion.

"We could have ruled the world together, Alejandro, and you're throwing it all away—for that little whore and her brat!"

Alejandro said softly, his face dangerous, "If you ever insult either my son or his mother again, you will regret it."

Claudie looked bewildered. To be fair, she'd insulted me for so long she'd probably forgotten it wasn't nice.

"But Alejandro…" Her voice had a strange begging sound I'd never heard from her. "You'll never find someone with my breeding, my beauty, my billions. I love you…."

"You love my title."

Her cheeks flushed red. "All right. But you can't choose her over me. She's…nothing. No one."

I swallowed, blinking fast.

"Blood always tells," she said. "She's not good enough for you."

Alejandro looked quickly at my miserable face. Then he turned back to Claudie with a deliberate smile.

"Thank you for your fascinating opinion. Now move, won't you? I need to take Lena shopping for an engagement ring."

"You're—what?" Claudie staggered back. I gasped. Miguel was crying.

The only one who looked absolutely calm was Alejandro. Turning away from her, he sat back in the plush leather seat, and said to Dowell, "Drive on."

Claudie stared after us, looking stupefied on the sidewalk, and almost forlorn in her tight club dress and bedraggled mascara. Looking back at her through the car window, I felt a strange wave of sympathy.

Because I, too, knew what it felt like to be left by Alejandro Navaro y Albra.

"You didn't have to be so cruel," I whispered.

"Cruel?" he said incredulously. "You defend her, after the way she treated you?"

"She's still my cousin. I feel sorry for her...."

"Then you're a fool," he said harshly.

I stroked my crying baby's cheek. My lips creased sadly. "Love makes us all fools."

"She doesn't love me. She doesn't even know me."

"That's what you said to me, too," I said softly. I met his gaze. "I wonder if any woman will ever truly know you."

For an instant, I thought I saw hunger, even

yearning in his dark eyes as he stared down at me. Then the expression shuttered, leaving me to decide I'd imagined it. But even then, he continued to look at me, as if he couldn't look away.

"What are you staring at?" I put my hand to my messy ponytail, feeling suddenly self-conscious. "I must look a mess."

"You look…" His eyes slowly traced over my hand, up my arm, to my neck, to my lips. "You look like a woman who cares more about her baby than a fortune. Like a woman who works so hard and so well—for free—that she's beloved by the entire household staff. You look," he said softly, "like a woman who feels sympathy, even for the coldhearted creature who tried to destroy her."

"Are you—complimenting me?"

He gave a low laugh. "If you're not sure, I must be losing my touch."

I flushed. Turning away, I took a deep breath. And changed the subject. "Thank you for bringing me back to London. For these." I motioned toward the photo albums. "And for giving me the chance to finally ask Claudie something I've wanted to know all my life. I always wondered why nothing I did was good enough to make her love me."

I looked out the window at the passing shops of Kensington High Street. "Now I know."

Silence fell.

"Are you all right?" he asked.

I nodded over the lump in my throat.

"I know how it feels," he said in a low voice, "to be alone."

"You?" I looked at him sharply, then gave a disbelieving snort. "No, you don't."

His dark eyes were veiled. "When I was young, I was good friends with…our housekeeper's son. We were only six months apart in age, and we studied under the same governess. Friend? He was more like a brother to me," he said softly. "People said we looked so much alike, acted so much alike, we could have been twins."

"Are you still friends?"

He blinked, focusing on me, and his jaw tightened. "He died in the same crash that took the duke, the duchess. The housekeeper. Twenty-three years ago."

"They all died in the same crash?" I said, horrified.

He looked down. "I was the only one to survive."

I thought of a young boy being the only survivor of a car accident that took his parents, his best friend. That made him a duke at the tender age of twelve. I couldn't even imagine the loneliness. The pain. Reaching out, I took his hand and whispered, "I'm sorry."

Alejandro drew away. "It was a long time ago." I saw tension in his jaw, heard it in his voice. "But I do know how it feels."

I swallowed, feeling guilty, and embarrassed, too, for all my complaining when he'd suffered worse, and in silence. "What was his name? Your friend?"

He stared at me, then his lips lifted slightly. "Miguel."

"Oh." I gave a shy smile. "So that's why you don't mind that I named our baby Miguel—"

"No." He seemed to hide his own private smile. "I don't mind at all."

I frowned, looking at him more closely.

His expression shuttered, and his dark eyebrows came down into a scowl. "His surname, however…"

I sighed. "I thought you might want to change that. But don't worry." I gave an awkward smile. "I won't hold you to your marriage proposal."

His eyes were dark and intense. "What if I want you to hold me to it?"

My lips parted in shock.

"What?" I said faintly.

His dark eyes challenged mine. "What if I want you to marry me?"

"You don't want to get married. You went on and on about all the women who tried to drag you to the altar. I'm not one of them!"

"I know that now." Leaning his arm across the baby seat, he cupped my cheek. "But for our son's sake, I'm starting to think you and I should be… together."

"Why?"

"Why not?" He gave a sensual smile. "As you said, I already broke one rule. Why not break the other?"

"But what has changed?"

"I'm starting to think…perhaps I can trust you." His eyes met mine. "And I can't forget how it felt to have you in my bed."

Something changed in the air between us. Something primal, dangerous. I felt the warmth of his palm against my skin and held my breath. As the limo drove through the streets of London, memories crackled through me like fire.

I remembered the night we'd conceived Miguel, and all the other hot days of summer, when I'd surrendered to him, body and soul. I trembled, feeling him so close in the backseat of the limo, on the other side of our baby. Every inch of my skin suddenly remembered the hot stroke of Alejandro's fingertips. My mouth was tingling, aching....

"That's not a good reason to marry someone. Especially for you. If I said yes, you'd regret it. You'd blame me. Claim that I'd only done it to be a rich duchess."

He slowly shook his head. "I think," he said quietly, "you might be the one woman who truly doesn't care about that. And it would be best for our son. So what is your answer?"

My answer?

I remembered the darkness I'd fallen into the last time Alejandro wanted me—then stopped wanting me. I'd never let myself be vulnerable to him ever again. I couldn't. He'd almost destroyed me once. I could never live through that again.

Sooner or later...he'll take your child and toss you in the gutter, like you deserve.

I couldn't give him control over me, ever again. I couldn't be tempted. My only hope was to get away. My only hope was...

Oh, heaven...what time was it?

"I need to…" As I saw the time on the dashboard of the limo, my heart nearly burst in panic. "Stop the car!" I leaned forward desperately toward the driver. "Let me out!"

Looking confused, Dowell pulled over on the side of the busy road.

"What are you doing?" Alejandro demanded, looking at me as if I was crazy. I felt crazy.

I unbuckled our baby, who'd just stopped crying and was looking drowsy. "Miguel needs a walk to help him sleep…."

"Is that a joke?"

I didn't answer. Cradling our baby, I stepped out on the sidewalk in front of Kensington Palace, and started running into the park, toward the playground. Toward Edward.

CHAPTER THREE

THE PRINCESS DIANA PLAYGROUND was in the corner of Kensington Gardens, just north of the palace. It was still early, and the playground had just opened, but in the midst of August holidays it was already starting to fill with children of every age, laughing and whooping as they raced toward the teepees and leaped on the ropes of the life-size pirate ship. It was a magical place, as you might expect of a children's playground, near a palace, based around a Peter Pan theme and named after a lost princess.

But I was here desperate for a different kind of magic.

Protection.

Edward St. Cyr had protected me more than once. We'd first properly met three years earlier, when I'd been walking up from the Tube late at night and I'd passed a group of rowdy teenagers on Kensington High Street. I'd been weighed down with groceries, and tried to keep my head down as they passed. But some of the boys had followed me up the dark street, taunting me crudely. As one started to knock the grocery bags out of my hand, there'd been a flash of headlights on the street and the slam of a car door, and suddenly a tall man in a dark coat was there, his face a threatening scowl, and the young men who'd scared me fled like rabbits into the snow. Then he'd turned to me.

"Are you all right, miss…?" Then his expression had changed. "But wait. I know you. You're Claudie Carlisle's cousin."

"Yes, I…"

"You're all right now." He'd gently taken my trembling hand. "I'm Edward St. Cyr. I live a few streets from here. May I give you a ride home?"

"No, I couldn't possibly. I…"

"I wouldn't mind a walk myself," he said briskly, and with a nod to the driver of his Rolls-Royce, he'd insisted on walking me home, though it took ten minutes.

"Thank you," I'd said at the door. "I never meant to impose…."

"You didn't." He'd paused. "I remember what it's like to feel alone and afraid. Will you let me check on you in the morning?"

I'd shaken my head. "It's truly not necessary."

"But you must." He'd lifted a dark eyebrow. "If for no other reason than it will annoy your cousin, whom I've despised for years. I insist."

Now, as I looked out at Kensington Gardens in the distance, I saw the paths where we'd once walked together, he and I. He'd been kind to me. We'd been—friends.

Or had we? Had he always wanted more?

I'm tired of waiting for you to forget that Spanish bastard. It's time for you to belong to me.

I shivered. When we left Mexico yesterday, I had been prepared to make any sacrifice to save my baby from Alejandro. Even if the price would have been going to bed with a man I did not love.

But now I was starting to wonder if that was truly necessary. Perhaps Alejandro was not entirely the heartless monster I'd once feared him to be....

"You shouldn't have run."

Hearing Alejandro's dark voice behind me, I whirled around. "How did you catch up so fast?"

He was scowling. "Did you think I'd let you disappear with Miguel?"

"I didn't disappear. I…"

"Had some kind of baby emergency?" He folded

his arms. "You ran for a reason. And we both know what it is."

Could he have somehow found out about Edward St. Cyr? The two men were slightly acquainted. And far from being friends. I didn't think he would take it well. I bit my lip, breathing, "I…"

"You panicked because I asked you to marry me," he accused.

Oh. I exhaled. "We both know you weren't serious."

"We both know I was."

"You won't be, once you have a chance to think about it. You don't want to get married. You said so a million times."

"I never intended to have a child, either," he pointed out, "so there was no reason to marry. But now… You heard what Claudie said. Marrying you will make clear to the whole world that he's my son. That he's my heir. Right or wrong," he said tightly.

Right or wrong? Meaning I wasn't good enough? That Miguel wasn't? My eyes narrowed. "I don't love you."

"I can live with that," he said sardonically. "We both love our son. That is the only love that matters."

"You're wrong," I said stubbornly. "My parents loved me, but they also loved each other, till the day they died. I remember how they looked at each other...."

"Most people are not so fortunate," he said harshly. "I've spent a year pursuing you, Lena. I don't want to fight over custody now. I don't want to worry, anytime you take him for a walk, that you might try to run away with him. I want this matter settled between us, once and for all."

Ah. Now we were getting down to it. "You mean I should give you total control over me, body and soul, so you can avoid the inconvenience of a custody battle?" I said incredulously, then shook my head. "This idea of marriage is just a momentary madness with you—it will pass...."

My voice trailed off as I saw Hildy on the edge of the playground, frantically signaling.

Alejandro frowned. "What is it?" He started to turn his head. "What are you..."

"On second thought, let me think it over," I said quickly. Touching his arm, I gave him a weak smile. "So much has happened since yesterday. Maybe I'm too exhausted to think straight." I pointed toward the outdoor café at the front of the playground. "Could you…please…get me some coffee?"

Alejandro's dark gaze flickered over my be-draggled dress, the dark circles under my eyes. "Of course, *querida,*" he murmured courteously. Turning away, he started toward the outdoor café.

The instant he was gone, I rushed to meet Hildy.

"Where's Edward?" I said desperately.

She was already shaking her head. "Mr. St. Cyr wasn't home. They said he's in Tokyo."

Of all the bad luck! "Can I borrow your phone?"

"Yes…." She reached into her pocket, then looked up, her mouth a round *O.* "I didn't bring it! It's still at home!"

Alejandro was already handing over money at the café. I saw him pick up two coffees from the counter. No time.

My shoulders fell. "Thanks anyway. You'd better go."

"Good luck, miss…."

Defeated, I looked out across the green park, deep emerald beneath the lowering gray London sky. I suddenly wondered what the weather was like in Spain. Warm. Sunny. Blue skies. With the chance of a hot, seductive Spaniard demanding that I share his bed.

No! I couldn't let myself think about it! Just sharing custody of Miguel would be bad enough. I would never, ever be Alejandro's lover! And certainly not his wife!

"Here." Alejandro handed me a white paper cup that warmed my hands. The coffee smelled like heaven. I took a sip, then sighed with appreciation as I felt the heat melt me from the inside. It was sweet, and creamy.

"You remembered how I liked it," I said in surprise.

He took a sip of his own black coffee, and gave a wicked grin. "That's how all women like it."

"That's not true!"

He shrugged. "It's mostly true. Cream and sugar will calm a woman down every time."

I glared at him. "You are such a—"

"A heartless bastard?" He paused, then tilted his head. "Do you still think I'll be such a disaster as a father?"

He sounded wistful, even—hurt? No. Impossible. A man like Alejandro had no heart to injure. But still, guilt rose in me, making my cheeks burn. "Maybe you're not *completely* evil." I looked down at the cup. "You did get my coffee right.

Even though you're completely wrong with your stereotype about women liking cream and sugar."

"Obviously," he agreed. He tilted his head. "Your arms must be getting tired from holding Miguel all this time."

"A bit," I admitted sheepishly. "He's starting to get too heavy to carry like this for long."

Finishing off his coffee, he threw the empty cup in the trash and reached out. "Give him to me."

I hesitated, then handed him over. I watched anxiously, but Alejandro was careful, holding him, even turning Miguel around so he could see the world around him. Alejandro caught my look. "How am I doing?"

"Not bad," I said grudgingly.

"Would you care to walk?" He lifted a dark eyebrow. "Since he needed a walk so badly that you almost jumped out of a moving car. This taking babies on walks must be a serious business. Or else you had some other reason for coming here that you don't want me to know about."

I looked at him sharply. Did he know something? Or was he just fishing?

He gave me a bland smile.

I shrugged. "It was what you said. Pure panic at your marriage proposal." I took a sip of coffee.

"Kind of like how you reacted last year when I told you I loved you. Instant disappearance." For a moment, we stared at each other. Then I turned away. "Yes. Let's walk."

The rain had eased up, and though gray skies were hovering, eager children of all ages, speaking many different languages, were now playing everywhere as we strolled past the pirate ship.

"So what is your answer?" he said casually, as if he'd been asking me out for a movie.

"About what?"

He looked at me.

"Oh." I licked my lips. "That."

"That."

"Be serious."

"I'm trying to be. But I've never asked any woman to marry me before. I'm starting to think I must be doing it wrong. Do I need to get down on one knee?"

"Don't you dare."

"Then what is it?"

I'm afraid you'd make me love you again. The cold knot near my heart, which had started to warm on the edges, returned to ice. "Come on," I mumbled, looking at the ground. "We both know that I'm not exactly duchess material."

"Are you trying to let me down gently?" he demanded. He stopped, leaning our baby against his hip as he looked at me. "Is there someone else? Perhaps the person who helped you flee London last year, and travel around the world?"

"It's not like that."

"When a man protects a woman," he said grimly, "it is exactly like that."

"How do you know it's a man?"

"By looking at your face," he said softly. "Right now."

I looked away. My throat hurt as I took another sip of the rich, sweet coffee, watching all the mothers and fathers and smiling nannies hovering on the edge of their children's delighted play. Some of them looked back at me. They probably imagined we were a family, too.

But we weren't.

I would have given anything if Alejandro could have been a man I could trust with my heart. A regular guy, a hardworking, loving man, who could have been my real partner. Instead of a selfish playboy duke who didn't know the meaning of love, and if married would plainly expect me to remain a dutiful wife imprisoned in his castle, raising our child, while he enjoyed himself elsewhere. Why shouldn't he? If love didn't exist, I could only imagine what he thought of fidelity.

"Why did you seduce me, Alejandro?" I blurted out.

He blinked. "What?"

My voice trembled as I looked up at him. "If you weren't trying to get me pregnant to provide an heir for you and Claudie, why did you seduce me? Why did you even notice me?"

"I don't understand."

"Are you really going to make me spell it out? Fine. You're—you—" I waved my half-full coffee toward him "—and I'm…" I indicated my white dress I'd worn for thirty-six hours now, wrinkled and possibly stained with baby sick I didn't know about, and I shivered in the cool morning air. "I believed Claudie's story last year because, for the first time, everything made sense. There was no other reason for you to… I mean, why else would a man like you, who could have any woman in the world, choose a woman like…"

Reaching out his hand, he cupped my cheek. "Because I wanted you, Lena. Pure and simple. I wanted you." Looking down at me, he said in a low voice, "I've never stopped wanting you."

My lips parted. I trembled, fighting the desire

to lean into his touch. The paper cup fell from my hand, splashing coffee across the grass. But I barely noticed. Craning back my head, I blinked back tears as I whispered, "Then why did you break up with me like that, so coldly and completely? Just for telling you I loved you?"

Alejandro stared at me, then dropped his hand. "Because I didn't want to lead you on. I'd promised myself I'd never have either wife or child...."

"But why?" I said, bewildered. "Why wouldn't you want those things? You're the last of your line, aren't you? If you died without an heir...you would be the last Duke of Alzacar."

"That was my intention," he said grimly.

"But why?"

"It doesn't matter anymore." He looked down at Miguel in his arms. "Fate chose differently. I have a son." His dark eyes blazed at me, filled with heat and anger and something else...something I couldn't understand. "And I will protect his future. Right or wrong."

"You keep saying *right or wrong*. What is wrong about it?" I narrowed my eyes. "If you're trying to imply that he's not good enough—"

"Of course not," he bit out.

"Then it's me—"

He shook his head impatiently, his jaw tight. "I'm talking about me."

The great Duque de Alzacar, admitting some kind of fault? I blinked. I breathed, "I don't understand...."

"What is there to understand?" he said evasively. "Now that I am a parent, my priorities have changed. Wasn't it the same for you, when Miguel was born?"

I hesitated. It was true what he said, but I still had the sense he was hiding something from me. "Yes-s...."

"We have a child. So we will do what is best for him. We will marry."

"You didn't want to marry me in Mexico."

"That was when I thought you were a liar, a thief and probably a gold digger. Now my opinion of you has improved."

"Thanks," I said wryly.

"Why are you fighting me? Unless—" He gave me a sharp, searching gaze. "Are you in love with someone else?"

The image of Edward flashed in front of my eyes. I wondered if Alejandro would still keep his improved opinion of me if he knew I'd been living in another man's house. It would look sordid, even if the truth had been so innocent. At least—innocent on my side. Swallowing, I looked away.

"I'm not in love with anyone." My voice was barely audible over the noisy children at play.

His shoulders relaxed imperceptibly. "Then why not marry me?" His tone turned almost playful. "You really should consider it for the jewels alone...."

I gave a rueful laugh, then looked at him. "I'd never fit into your world, Alejandro. If I took you at your word and became your wife, we'd both be miserable."

"I wouldn't be."

I shook my head. "Your expectations of marriage are lower than mine. It would never work. I want—" I looked down as my cheeks turned hot "—to be loved. I want what my parents had."

Alejandro abruptly stopped. We were in the far back of the playground now, in a quiet overgrown place of bushes and trees. "But what about our son? Doesn't he have some rights, as well? Doesn't he deserve a stable home?"

"You mean a cold, drafty castle?"

"It's neither drafty nor cold." He set his jaw. "I want my son, my heir, to live in Spain. To know his people. His family."

I frowned at him. "I thought you had no family."

"My grandmother who raised me. All the people on my estate. They are like family to me. Don't you think he deserves to know them, and they should know him? Shouldn't he know his country? Where else would you take him—back to Mexico?"

"I loved it there!" I said, stung.

"We will buy a vacation house there," he said impatiently. "But his home is with his land. With his people. With his parents. You of all people," he said softly, "know what it means to have a happy, settled childhood, surrounded by love."

I sucked in my breath. I felt myself wavering. Of course I wanted all those things for my son.

"You'll be a duchess, honored, wealthy beyond imagining."

"I'd be the poor stupid wife sitting at home in the castle," I whispered, hardly daring to meet his gaze, "while you were out having a good time with other, more glamorous women...."

His dark eyes narrowed. "I have many faults, but disloyalty is not one of them. Still, I can understand why you'd immediately think of cheating. Tell me—" he moved closer, his sardonic gaze sweeping over me "—did you enjoy having the use of Edward St. Cyr's house? His jet?"

My eyes went wide. My mouth suddenly went dry.

"How did you find out?" I said weakly.

"Before my jet left Mexico, I told my investigators to dig into the layer of the shell company that owned the house in San Miguel. If it wasn't Claudie who helped you," he said grimly, "I intended to find out who it really was."

Well. That explained why he'd stopped asking. "Why have you pretended all day you didn't know?"

His handsome face looked chiseled and hard as marble beneath the gray sky. "I wanted to give you the chance to tell me."

"A test?" I whispered.

"If you like." His eyes glittered. "Women always find the quality of danger so attractive. Until they find out what *danger* really means. Tell me. Did you enjoy using St. Cyr's possessions? His money? His jet? How about his bed? Did you enjoy sharing that?"

"I never shared his bed!" I tried not to remember the husky sound of Edward's voice. *It's time for you to belong to me.* Or the way he'd flinched at my reaction—an incredulous, unwilling laugh. He'd taken a deep breath. *You'll see,* he'd whispered, then turned and left. Pushing the memory away, I lifted my chin. "We've never even kissed!"

"I see." Lifting an eyebrow, Alejandro said scornfully, "He helped you out of the goodness of his heart."

That might be pushing it. I bit my lip. "Um… yes?"

"Is that a statement or a question?"

"He's a friend to me," I whispered. "Just a friend."

Alejandro looked at me more closely. "But he wants more, doesn't he?" The sweep of his dark lashes left a shadow against his olive skin, his taut cheekbones, as he looked down at our baby in his arms. After all this time, he still carried Miguel as if he were no weight at all. He said in a low voice, "I won't let my son keep such company. Because I, at least, have clear eyes about what *danger* means."

"And I understand at last," I choked out, "why you suddenly want to marry me."

He narrowed his eyes at me. "Lena—"

"You say he is dangerous? Maybe he is. But if it weren't for Edward St. Cyr, I don't think I could have survived the darkness and fear of the past year. He was there for me when you deserted me. When you left me pregnant and alone and afraid."

His face turned white, then red. "If you'd given me the chance—"

"I did give you a chance. You never called me back." I took a deep breath. "I know now you weren't the monster I thought you were. But I'll never be able to trust you like I did. It's lost. Along with the way I loved you."

Silence fell, the only sound the children playing on the other side of the trees. I heard their shrieks of joy.

When Alejandro spoke, his voice was low, even grim. "Love me or not, trust me or not, but you will marry me. Miguel will have a stable family. A real home."

I shook my head. He moved closer.

"You promised to come to Spain, Lena," he said. "You gave your word."

I threw him a panicked glance. "That was when—"

"Ah. You hoped you could break your promise, didn't you? Perhaps with St. Cyr's help?"

My silence spoke volumes. His dark eyes hardened. "You gave me your word that if I brought you to London, you would come with me to Spain."

He was right. I had. Now, I felt so alone and forlorn. Alejandro was starting to wear me down. To break my will. To remind me of a promise I'd never wanted to keep.

"It will only lead to misery," I whispered.

"Wherever it leads," he said softly, "whatever we'd once planned for our lives…you are part of my family now."

"Your family. You mean your grandmother?" I shivered, imagining a coldly imperious grande dame in pearls and head-to-toe vintage Chanel. A little like my own grandmother, in fact. "She will hate me. She'll never think I'm good enough."

He gave a low laugh. "You think you know what to expect? A cold, proud dowager in a cold, drafty castle?"

"Am I wrong?"

"My grandmother was born in the United States. In Idaho. The daughter of Basque sheep ranchers."

"Idaho?" My mouth fell open. "How did she…?"

"How did she end up married to my grandfather? It is an interesting story. Perhaps you can ask her when you meet her." His lips twisted grimly. "Unless you intend to break your promise, and refuse to go to Spain after all."

I swallowed, afraid of what it would mean to go to his castle. Surrounded by his family and friends. Surrounded by his *power*. How long could I resist his marriage demand then?

"Enough. You always spend too long in your mind, going back and forth on decisions that have already been made. End it now." Reaching into his pocket, Alejandro pulled out a phone and dialed a number. He pushed it into my hand. "It's ringing."

"What?" I stammered, staring down at the phone. "Whom did you call?"

"My grandmother. If you are breaking your promise to me, if you are truly not willing to bring Miguel to Spain to meet her, tell her now."

"Me? I can't talk to your grandmother!"

"No. *I* can't," he said coldly, "because I love her. *You* have no feelings for her whatsoever, so you should have no trouble being cruel."

"You think I'm cruel?" I whispered as the phone rang.

His eyes met mine. "Tell her she has a great-grandchild. Introduce yourself. Tell her I've asked you to marry me. Go on."

I stared at him numbly, then heard a tremulous voice at the other end of the line.

"*¿Hola?* Alejandro?"

It was a warm, sweet, kindly voice, the sort of voice that a grandmother would have in a movie, the grandmother who bakes cookies and is plump and white-haired and gives you hugs and tells you to eat more pie—or in this case, more paella?—because food is love, and she loves you so much that you're her whole existence, her light, her star. It was the type of voice I had not heard since my parents had died.

"Alejandro?" The woman sounded worried now. "Are you there?"

"It's not Alejandro," I replied, my voice unsteady. "But he asked me to call you. I'm a... friend."

"A friend?" The sweet tremulous voice gasped, her accent definitely American. "Has he fallen sick? Was he in an accident?"

"No, he's fine...."

"If he were fine, he'd be calling me himself, as he always does." A sob choked her voice. "You're trying to break it to me gently. But you can't. First I lost my children, then my..." Her voice broke. "Alejandro was all I had left. I always knew I would lose him someday. That sooner or later—" another sob "—fate would catch up with me and…"

"Oh, for heaven's sake!" I cried in exasperation. "Alejandro's fine! He's standing right by me!"

She sucked in her breath. Her tone changed, became curious. "Then why are you calling me on his phone?"

"He…wanted me to tell you the happy news." Glaring at Alejandro, I kept my voice gentle as I said, "You're a great-grandmother."

"A—" her voice ended in a gasp. A happy gasp. "Alejandro has a child?"

"We have a five-month-old son. I'm the baby's mother."

"You're American? Canadian?"

"Born in Brooklyn."

"Why didn't he tell me before? What's your name? Have we met?" She didn't seem like the snooty duchess I'd imagined. She continued eagerly, "Did you elope? Oh, I'll never forgive Alejandro for getting married without me—"

"He didn't tell you because—well, he wasn't sure about it. For your other question, we're not married." I gritted my teeth. "And we have no plans to be."

"You have no—" She cut herself off with an intake of breath. Then changing the subject with forced cheer, she said, "So when can I meet my great-grandson? I can hardly wait to tell my friends you're coming to live in the castle. The pitter-patter of little feet at Rohares Castle at last!"

"I'm sorry. We're not going to live in Spain."

"Oh." I heard the soft whoosh of her whimper. "That's…all right." She took a deep breath. "So when are you coming to visit so I can meet him?"

I bit my lip. "I don't know if we can…."

"I understand," she sniffled. "It's fine. Just send me a Christmas card with the baby's picture, and…it's fine. I've had a good life. I don't need to meet my only great-grandchild…."

My own fear of spending time with Alejandro, of allowing him more power over me, suddenly felt small and selfish compared with letting her meet Miguel—and even more important, allowing my son to have the family I myself had yearned for. What did I have, a heart of stone?

"All right." With a sigh, I accepted the inevitable. "We'll come to Spain in the next day or two. Just for a visit, mind!"

But even with that warning, her cries of joy exploded from the phone. I held it away from my ear, glaring all the while at Alejandro. "I'll let you talk to Alejandro," I told her, then covering the mouthpiece, I handed him the phone and grumbled, "I hate you."

"No, you don't." He took it from my hand, looking down at me seriously. "I'll win your trust, Lena. And then…"

"Then?"

He gave me a sensual smile. "You'll be my wife within the week."

There are many different kinds of seduction.

There's the traditional kind, with flowers, chocolates, dinner by candlelight. That's the way Alejandro had seduced me last summer. He called the Kensington mansion, asked for me, invited me to dinner. He showed up at the door dressed in a tux, his arms full of roses—to Claudie's rage—and greeted me with a chaste kiss on the cheek.

"You look beautiful," he'd murmured, and took me to the best restaurant in London. He asked me questions, listened aptly and physically grew closer and closer, with the innocent touch of his hand, the casual brush of his body against mine. He held my hand across the dinner table in the candlelight, in full view of the other patrons, looking at me with deep soulful eyes, as if no other woman had ever existed. Afterward, he took me to a club. We danced, and he pulled me into his arms, against his hard, powerful body. Closer. Closer still, until my heart was in my throat and I started to feel dizzy. In the middle of the dance floor, he lowered his head and kissed me for the first time.

It was my first kiss, and as I closed my eyes I felt the whole world whirling around me. Around us.

When he finally pulled away, he whispered against my skin, "I want you." I'd trembled, my heart beating violently, like a deer in a wolf's jaws. He'd looked down at me and smiled. Then took me back to his rooftop terrace suite at the Dorchester Hotel.

There had been no question of resistance. I was a virgin in the hands of a master. He'd had me from the moment he kissed me. From the moment he showed up at my door in a sleek tuxedo, with his arms full of roses, and told me he wanted me in his low, husky voice. He'd had me from the moment he'd seared me with the intensity of his full attention.

That was the traditional way of seduction. It had worked once, worked with utterly ruthless efficiency against my unprepared heart. But I knew the moves now—that is to say, I knew how they ended. With pleasure that was all too brief, and agony that was all too long.

But there are many different kinds of seduction.

Alejandro had decided we wouldn't leave immediately for Madrid, but would spend one night in London, resting at his usual suite of rooms at the Dorchester. He told me it was because the baby and I both looked tired. I was immediately suspicious, but as we left the park, he did not try to kiss me. Even after we'd arrived at the luxurious hotel, he did not look deeply into my eyes and tell me I was the most beautiful woman on earth, or pull me out onto the rooftop terrace, overlooking Hyde Park and all the wide gray sky, to take me in his arms.

Instead, he just ordered us lunch via room service, then afterward, he smiled at me. "We need to go shopping."

I frowned at him, suspecting a trick. "No, we don't."

"We do need a stroller," he said innocently. "A pushcart. For the baby."

I could hardly argue with that, since we'd left

the umbrella stroller back in San Miguel. "Fine,"
I grumbled. "A stroller. That's it."

"You're very boring."

"I'm broke."

"I'm not."

"Lucky you."

"I can buy you things, you know."

"I don't want you to."

"Why?"

I set my jaw. "I'm afraid what they'd cost me."

He just answered with an innocent smile, and
had his driver take us to the best shops in Knights-
bridge, Mayfair and Sloane Street. He bought the
most expensive pushcart he could find for Miguel,
then pushed it himself, leaving the bodyguards
trailing behind us to hold only shopping bags full
of clothes and toys for the baby.

"You said just a stroller!"

"Surely you wouldn't begrudge me the chance
to buy a few small items for my son?"

"No," I sighed. But Alejandro kept pushing the
boundaries. All the bodyguards who trailed us
were soon weighed down with shopping bags.

"Now we must get you some clothes, as well,"
Alejandro said, smiling as he caught me look-

ing wistfully at the lovely, expensive dresses. I jumped, then blushed guiltily.

"No. Absolutely not."

"It's the least I can do," Alejandro replied firmly, "considering it was because of me that you lost your inheritance."

"That wasn't your fault..." I protested. He looked down at me with his big, dark, Spanish eyes.

"Please let me do this, *querida*. I must," he said softly. "Such a small thing. You cannot deny me my desire."

I shivered. That was exactly what I was afraid of. That if I couldn't deny him this, I wouldn't be able to deny him anything. And soon I'd be putty in his hands again, like a spaniel waiting for her master with slippers in her mouth.

I'd end up married to a man who didn't love me. Who would ignore me. And I'd spend the rest of my life like a ghost, haunting his stupid castle.

Wordlessly, I shook my head. He sighed, looking sad.

I was proud of myself for sticking to my guns. But as we walked through the expensive shops, Alejandro saw me looking at a pretty dress a second too long. He gave one of his bodyguards a glance, and the man snatched it up in my size.

"What!" I exclaimed. "No. I don't want that!"

"Too bad," he said smugly. "I just bought it for you."

Irritated, I tried to foil Alejandro's plan by carefully *not* looking at any of the beautiful clothes, shoes or bags as we walked through the luxury department store and designer boutiques. But that didn't work, either. He simply started picking things out for me, items far more expensive and flashy than I would have picked out for myself. Instead of the black leather quilted handbag I might have chosen, I found myself suddenly the owner of a handbag in crocodile skin with fourteen-karat-gold fittings and diamonds woven into the chain.

"I can't wear that!" I protested. "I'd look a proper fool!"

He grinned. "If you don't like me choosing for you, you have to tell me what you want."

So I did. I had no choice.

"Dirty blackmailer," I grumbled as I picked out a simple cotton sweater from Prada, but his smile only widened.

The salespeople, sensing blood in the water,

left their previous customers to follow eagerly in our wake. The size of our entourage quickly exploded, with salespeople, bodyguards, Alejandro, me and our baby in a stroller so expensive that it, too, might as well have been made of rare leathers and solid gold. Other people turned their heads to watch as we went by, their eyes big as they whispered to each other beneath their hands.

"I feel conspicuous," I complained to Alejandro.

"You deserve to be looked at," he said. "You deserve everyone's attention."

I was relieved to return to his suite of rooms at the Dorchester, even though it was so fancy, the same suite Elizabeth Taylor had once lived in. I was happy to be alone with him.

And yet not happy.

It took a long time for the bodyguards to bring up all the packages. Even with help from the hotel staff.

"I didn't realize we bought so much," I said, blushing.

Alejandro gave a low laugh as he tipped the staff then turned back. "You hardly bought anything. I would have given you far more." He looked down at me. Running his hand beneath my jaw, he said softly, "I want to give you more."

We stood together, alone in the living room of the suite, and I held my breath. Praying he wouldn't kiss me. Wishing desperately that he would.

But with a low laugh, he released me. "Are you hungry?"

After I fed Miguel and tucked him to bed in the second bedroom, we had an early dinner in the dining room, beneath a crystal chandelier, on an elegant table that would seat eight, with a view not just of London, but of the exact place where, last summer, he'd pressed me against the silver wallpaper and made love to me, hot and fast and fierce against the wall.

All through dinner, I tried not to look at that wall. Or think about the bed next door.

I told myself he wasn't trying to seduce me. Maybe he wasn't. Maybe it was just my delusion, reading desire in his dark, hot glances. It had to be me. He wouldn't actually be intending to…

Alejandro suddenly smiled at me. "You are tired. It has been a long day for you."

"All that shopping," I grumbled. He grinned, taking an innocent sip of his after-dinner coffee.

"I meant before that. Mexico. Claudie. Your sleepless night on the plane…"

"Oh." I yawned, as if on cue. "I am a little tired."

"So go take some time for yourself. Take a nap. A shower. Go to bed. I will take over."

"Take over?"

"With Miguel." As I blinked at him in confusion, he lifted a dark eyebrow and added mildly, "Surely you can trust me that far—as far as the next room? If there is any problem, I will wake you. But there won't be. Go rest."

I took a long, hot shower, and it was heaven. Putting on a soft new nightgown straight from the designer bag, I fell into the large bed, knowing that someone else was watching our child as I slept, and I wasn't on call. That was the most deliciously luxurious thing of all.

When I woke, early-morning sunlight was streaking across the large bed, where I'd clearly slept alone. Looking at the clock, I saw to my shock I'd slept twelve hours straight—my best night's sleep in a year. I stretched in bed, yawning, feeling fantastic. Feeling grateful. Alejandro...

Alejandro!

He couldn't possibly have stayed up all night with the baby! He must have left. Jumping out of bed in panic, I flung open the bedroom door, terrified that Alejandro had spirited away our baby and left me behind.

But Alejandro was in the living room, walking our baby back and forth, singing a Spanish song in his low, deep voice, as Miguel's eyes grew heavy. Then Alejandro saw me, and he gave me a brilliant smile, even though his eyes, too, looked tired.

"*Buenos días, querida.* Did you sleep?"

"Beautifully," I said, running my hands through my hair, suddenly self-conscious of my nightgown, which in this bright morning light looked like a slinky silk negligee. I tried to casually cover the outline of my breasts with my arms. "And you?"

"Ah," he said, smiling tenderly down at his son. "For us, it is still a work in progress. But by the time we are on the plane to Madrid, after breakfast, I think our little man will sleep. He's worn himself out, haven't you?"

I stared at the two of them together, the strong-shouldered Spaniard holding his tiny son so lovingly, with such infinite care and patience, though he'd clearly kept Alejandro up most of the night.

Miguel looked up with big eyes at his father. They had the same face, though one was smaller and chubby, the other larger and chiseled at the cheekbones and jaw. But I could not deny the look of love that glowed from Alejandro's eyes as he looked into the face of his son.

I'd been wrong, I realized. Alejandro did know how to love.

He just didn't know how to love *me.*

Turning back, Alejandro gave me a big grin, filled with joy and pride. Our eyes locked.

The smile slowly slid from his face. I felt his gaze from my head to my toes and everywhere in between. His soulful dark eyes seemed to last forever, like those starlit summer nights.

I looked at Alejandro in this moment, and I was suddenly afraid. Seeing him as a father, as a true partner in caring for the tiny person I loved so much, I trembled.

I could handle his gifts. I might even be able to handle the sensual awareness that electrified the air between us. I could keep my heart on ice. I could resist.

But this?

There are many different kinds of seduction. Some are of the body. Some are of the mind.

But others, the most powerful, are of the heart.

CHAPTER FOUR

I'M NOT GOING to lie. A private jet makes travel easier. Especially with a baby. We had a quick flight from London to Madrid. No standing in lines, no fighting for overhead space. And I felt much better than I had on the last flight. I was well slept, showered. My hair was brushed until it tumbled over my shoulders. I'd even put on a little mascara. Arriving in Madrid in my new soft pink blouse and form-fitting jeans, I felt almost pretty.

"Where's your diamond handbag?" Alejandro teased as we left the jet, going down the steps to the tarmac of the private airport, followed by his men carrying our luggage. "Don't you like it?"

I bit my lip. "Well…"

He put his hand on his heart, as if it had been stabbed with grief. "You don't!"

"Don't worry," I assured him. "I'll still use it. I was needing a new diaper bag."

He gave a low laugh, then sobered, his dark eyes

resting on mine as he said softly, "I'll have to see if I can find some other gift to please you more."

I shivered at his glance, then looked out the window of the SUV. *He's not trying to seduce me,* I repeated silently to myself. *He's not. He's just trying to lure me into a loveless marriage of convenience—don't fall for it, don't...*

Madrid was beautiful, an elegant, formal city with its nineteenth-century architecture, spreading regally across the banks of the Manzanares River. All the gray clouds of San Miguel and London seemed a million miles away. Here, the August sky was bright blue, and the Spanish sun burning hot.

Alejandro's driver took us to his penthouse apartment near the Prado, the bodyguards and luggage following in the car behind. We arrived at the flat, which took the entire top floor, and were answered at the door by a middle-aged woman who seemed far too young to be his grandmother. He quickly introduced her as his longtime housekeeper, the only paid staff at the penthouse, Mrs. Gutierrez, who lived on a floor below.

Alejandro walked us around the enormous apartment, with its stark contemporary furnishings and enormous windows overlooking the city. "What do you think?"

"It's beautiful," I said slowly, "but so cold. You can hardly tell anyone lives here." Shivering, I cuddled my warm baby close. "You must not stay here much."

He blinked. "More blunt honesty."

"Was I rude?"

"I can take it." He shifted his weight, then clawed back his thick, dark hair. I wondered what it would feel like to… No! I stopped the thought cold. Oblivious of my inner struggle, he continued with a sigh, "My company is headquartered here. I am in Madrid all the time."

"Oh," I said, looking at all the sharp edges of the furniture, all the glass and chrome. "Um. Well. It's very—masculine."

He lifted a dark eyebrow. "Perhaps it needs a woman's touch."

In my current frame of mind, I wondered if he was talking about more than his apartment. My cheeks went hot and I cleared my throat. "I'm surprised your grandmother isn't here. She sounded so keen to meet her great-grandson."

"You'll meet her tomorrow. I have an event tonight in Madrid, and Abuela doesn't like to leave her roses, or all the people who count on her at the castle."

"The castle?"

"Rohares, near Seville. Where the Dukes of Alzacar have lived for four hundred years."

"Cold and drafty," I sighed.

"Exactamente." He gave me a sideways glance, seeming to hide a smile. "I can hardly wait for you to see it."

"Yeah," I grumbled. "How many rooms?"

"I lose count," he said, and I couldn't tell if he was joking. But at least such a large building would create more space between us. Even this large penthouse felt too…close, when we were together. Every glance, every word, made me more attracted. It was dangerous.

As soon as his grandmother met the baby, I told myself firmly, I'd be out of this country and away from Alejandro. We'd come to some agreement over custody. Preferably one that involved Miguel living with me in Mexico.

Although it would be a shame to separate my son from a father who loved him, just because I was afraid of being hurt….

I pushed the thought away. "You said something about an event tonight?"

"A celebration—a ball, really. Hosted by my company. Starts in—" he glanced at his platinum watch and said calmly "—twenty minutes."

Thank heavens! I wouldn't have to spend the evening with him, trying desperately not to feel tempted! With real relief, I said, "Go and have a good time. We'll be fine. I'll tuck Miguel into bed and maybe read a book until…"

But he was already shaking his head. "Leave you alone with our son, giving you the opportunity to run away again? No."

"Why do you think I'd run away?"

"Why would I think you wouldn't?"

"You could post your bodyguards at the door," I suggested.

"You'd charm them and escape."

He thought I was charming? For an instant I felt flattered. Then I folded my arms. "You could just decide to trust me."

"I will trust you." He tilted his head, looking down at me with amusement. "As soon as you marry me."

"Never going to happen, and believe me, after this momentary madness—or whatever it is—passes, you'll thank me."

"Fine," he sighed, plunking down on the soft

sofa in front of a wide-screen TV and a window with a view of the city. He reached for the remote control. "Shall we see if there are any good movies on tonight? Maybe order takeaway?"

I stared at him, my lips parted. "You can't miss your own party."

He shrugged. "Yes. It's a pity. Especially since it was to celebrate my company's upcoming IPO on the stock exchange. But I can miss it to watch a TV movie with you. No problem."

"Are you crazy? You can't miss something like that. You're the host! If you don't even bother showing up, what do you think it will do to your stock price?"

"It's fine. Really." He shrugged. "I don't have a date to the ball anyway."

"You honestly expect me to believe you don't have a date—*you?*"

"You have to admit it's kind of your fault."

Now we were getting down to it.

"How is it my fault?" I said suspiciously.

Tilting his head, he looked at me from the sofa. "I *did* have a date for tonight." He stroked his chin thoughtfully. "A beautiful Swedish swimsuit model, in fact. But when I called her yesterday and explained I wouldn't be picking her up in my jet because I'd just discovered a former mistress had my baby and I had to spend the day buying you presents instead of flying to Stockholm to collect her, well—for some reason, Elsa wasn't interested in flying coach to Madrid to be my date tonight."

I hid a laugh, tried to look mad. "Too bad for you. But it's really not my problem."

He nodded sagely. "You're scared."

"Scared? Of what?"

"Of spending time with me. You're scared you'll be overwhelmed with desire and say yes to everything, and wake up tomorrow morning, in my bed, with a ring on your finger."

In his *bed?* My mouth went dry.

"It's all right. I understand." He fluttered his dark eyelashes outrageously. "You don't trust yourself, because you want me so badly."

It was so true. "That's so not true!"

He lifted his eyebrows. "Then you'll be my date?"

I thought about the type of people I'd be likely to meet at his party. A bunch of wealthy, beautiful, *mean* people. Just like Claudie. "No, thanks."

"Why?" he demanded.

"The baby will wake up at midnight for a feeding..." I said weakly.

"I'll have you back by midnight. Via pumpkin coach if necessary."

"There's no one I can trust as his babysitter!"

"Mrs. Gutierrez raised four children, and has ten grandchildren. She's very trustworthy and experienced, and she's agreed to stay."

"You thought of everything," I grumbled.

"So say yes."

"I won't fit in with your friends, okay?"

"Always so afraid," he sighed. "Of me. Of them. Of your own shadow."

He was clearly taunting me, but I couldn't help but bristle. "Even if I wanted to go with you, it's too late. Your party starts in twenty minutes, and unless you bought a ball gown in London yesterday without me noticing, I have nothing to wear!"

Alejandro smiled. "Did I ever show you our bedroom?"

I shook my head with a scowl. "It's either yours or mine. Not *ours*."

"That's what I meant," he said innocently. Walking ahead in the hallway, he pushed open a door.

The bedroom was enormous, with an amazing

view of Madrid, but sparsely furnished, with only an expensive, masculine bed. And, incongruously, a crib beside it.

But when I looked closer at the bed, I saw a flash of pink. Coming closer, I gasped when I saw a pale pink gown, a delicious confection of flowers and silk, spread across his plain white bedspread. I picked it up with one hand, then dropped it when I saw the tag peeking at me. Oscar de la Renta.

A pumpkin coach, indeed! I whirled to face him. "You bought this yesterday. You always intended to bring me as your date tonight," I accused.

His lips were curved in a sensual smile, then his hands went up in mock surrender. "I admit it." Then he put down his hands, and his expression changed. His dark eyes became intent. Sensual. "I always get what I want," he said softly, searching my gaze. "And I don't give up. When something is difficult to possess, that only makes me want it more."

For a long heartbeat, we stared at each other in his bedroom.

Then I tossed my head, hoping he couldn't see how my body was trembling. "Fine. Have it your way. I'll come with you tonight, since it means so much to you. I'll do it for Miguel's sake, so your friends will know he wasn't just the result of some cheap one-night stand. But that's it."

His dark eyes burned into mine. "A cheap one-night stand? That is the last thing you were to me. You should know that by now."

A shiver went down my spine and through my soul. I straightened, locking my knees, and I handed him the baby. "I'll get dressed as quickly as I can."

Thirty minutes later, Alejandro helped me out of the limo, holding my hand as we walked up a red carpet, past the flashbulbs of the paparazzi.

"I thought your company was a metals and real estate conglomerate," I murmured beneath all of the attention.

"It is," he said innocently, "among other things. We recently bought a movie studio. Look." I followed his gaze to see a beautiful movie star whom I'd admired for years just ahead of us in a tight sequined gown. "That's the reason for the paparazzi."

"She is beautiful," I said.

He looked down at me. "You're more beautiful than her on your worst day. Even when you are wearing a dress like a sack and barely brush your hair."

I snorted, expecting mockery. "You are so full of—"

Then I saw his expression, the frank hunger in his eyes as he looked at me, and my mouth went dry.

"Come on," he said roughly. "The sooner we get this done, the sooner we can go home."

I licked my lips, tasting lipstick, which was foreign to me. But in this pale pink ball gown, I didn't feel like myself at all. I might as well have been wearing glass slippers....

Alejandro led me into a large ballroom, filled with people dancing and drinking champagne beneath enormous crystal chandeliers high overhead. I watched as, ten minutes after we arrived, he went to the elevated dais and made a short speech into a microphone, congratulating the staff of his company, and thanking all their investors and friends, which was met by a roar of applause. When he left the microphone, he returned to my side.

"Now the work is done," he whispered, nuzzling my ear. "Let's have some fun."

He took me out on the dance floor, and I trembled, remembering the last time he'd held me in his arms on a dance floor, the way he'd slowly seduced me, until I surrendered in my first kiss. Now, I felt his arms around me, and I shuddered from deep within, feeling his warmth and strength beneath the tuxedo, breathing in his cologne and the scent that was uniquely him. When the music ended after the first dance, I pulled away.

"I—I need some champagne," I said unsteadily.

"Of course," he said huskily, his dark eyes intent, as if he saw through me, every inch and pore, down to my heart and soul.

For the rest of the night, Alejandro was the perfect gentleman, solicitous, getting me champagne, even cheerfully introducing me to the acquaintances who quickly surrounded us.

One of his friends, a German tycoon of some kind, looked me over appreciatively. "Where did you keep this beautiful creature hidden, Your Excellency?"

"Yes, you should have introduced us," a handsome Japanese millionaire said.

"You sure you want this guy, Miss Carlisle?" An actor I recognized from a big summer movie, where he'd gotten revenge against aliens who blew up Paris, gave me a big shiny grin. "You haven't given the rest of us a chance yet."

I blushed. The whole night seemed unreal, as if I were playing a part, with my hair pulled back into a high ballerina bun, wearing the petal-pink ball gown with tiny flowers embroidered over it. Remembering the part I was to play, I glanced at Alejandro. "Sorry. I only want Alejandro."

His relief was palpable. He smiled back at me.

"Awww, so sweet," the movie star said, somewhat ironically. "Well. Whenever the romance is over, feel free to…"

"It's not a romance," a man said behind us. "It's extortion."

Turning, I sucked in my breath. A man stood behind us, dressed exactly like the others, in a sharp black tuxedo. The man I'd been so desperate to see—and yet, oddly, he seemed out of place here. Handsome. But malevolent.

"Edward," I breathed. "I thought you were in Tokyo—"

His eyes softened. "My staff called me. I was glad to hear you'd gone to London to see me. But not so glad to hear who was with you." He glared at Alejandro, his jaw tight, even as he continued to speak to me. "Are you all right?"

"Of course I'm all right," I said, suddenly nervous.

The two men were glaring at each other, both of them straining the size of the ballroom between their shoulders and masculine pride. I had a sudden dismaying flash of two predators, growling over the same female—or the same prey.

Alejandro's eyes narrowed, but with a swift glance at me, he politely put out his hand. "Edward St. Cyr. I know you by reputation, of course."

The words were courteous and cool. Edward took them as the insult they were no doubt intended. Without taking the offered hand, he bared his teeth in a smile. "How gracious of you to say so. I know of you not just from reputation, but also from more…personal sources." He looked down dismissively at Alejandro's hand. "It does seem a little…tacky?…that after dragging Lena to Europe, you'd force her to pose as your date."

"I didn't force her."

"Of course you did," he said roughly. "What is it, some feeble attempt to project stability for the benefit of future shareholders? Or—no, don't tell me—some attempt to make her love you again?" Smiling his shark's smile, Edward held up his glass of champagne in salute. "You'd think destroying her once would be enough for you. But if anyone would be selfish enough to try for twice, it's you, Navaro."

No respectful *Your Excellency*. Just Alejandro's surname, tossed out with scorn. The entire group, including me, stared wide-eyed as Edward drank down the entire contents of his champagne glass. We looked at Alejandro.

He had dropped his hand, his eyelids now narrowed to slits. "Whatever you might have heard about me, it was a mistake." He glanced at me. "Lena now knows the truth."

Edward lifted an eyebrow. "Convinced her of that, have you?"

"What are you even doing here?" Alejandro's face hardened. "I don't recall sending you an invitation."

Setting his empty glass down on a nearby tray, Edward looked over the ballroom with a small smile. "I have plenty of friends. One was happy to bring me along."

"Who?"

"The Bulgarian ambassador." Edward turned back with lifted eyebrows and said mildly, "Surely you're not going to throw us out and risk an international incident?"

Alejandro looked at a gray-haired, distinguished-looking man across the ballroom, who appeared deep in conversation with someone I recognized from newspaper photos, who'd recently won the Nobel Peace Prize. He turned back with gritted teeth. "What do you want, St. Cyr?"

"I want Lena, since she's asked for me," he said softly. He turned to me, holding out his arm. "Shall we go, love?"

I heard a low, almost barbaric growl, and suddenly Alejandro was in front of me, blocking me from Edward's outstretched arm.

"So it's like that, is it?" Edward said. "She's your prisoner?"

"She's here with me of her own free will."

"*Free will.*" Edward's lips pulled back, revealing white, sharp teeth. "Meaning you probably blackmailed her over that baby. You have no real claim on her."

"I have every claim."

"Because she had your child?" He snorted, jerking his chin. "Keep it," he said derisively. "If I'm the man she wants, I will give her more."

I gasped aloud at his cold reference to Miguel. *It?*

Edward couldn't have referred to my precious baby as "it." He couldn't have implied that he could get me pregnant and replace Miguel in my arms, in my life, as easily as someone might replace a new shoe.

Could he?

The black slash of Alejandro's eyebrows lowered. Every line of his hard-muscled body was taut, as if he were barely holding back from attack. He reminded me of a lion, or a wolf, coiled to spring, with only a thin veneer of civilized reason holding him in check—but not for much longer.

The two of them were about to start a brawl. Right here, in this elegant gilded ballroom, surrounded by the glitterati of Spain and all the world. The crowd around us was already growing, and so were the whispers. I wished I'd never started this by trying to contact Edward. Desperately, I yanked on his sleeve. "Please. Don't…"

Edward looked down at me condescendingly. "It's all right, Lena. I'm here now. I won't let him bully you." His eyes were hard, and his broad shoulders were square, like a rugby player's. And the condescending smile he gave me, after the cold, contemptuous stare he'd just given Alejandro, made me wish he was a million miles away. "You're safe. I'll take over."

"*Take over?*" I repeated incredulously.

Just yesterday, I'd wished so ardently for Edward's help. I'd remembered only that a year ago, when I'd needed to escape London, when I'd felt desperate and terrified and alone, I'd been grateful for his strength. But now...

I'd forgotten what Edward was really like.

Forgotten the times he'd visited his house in Mexico after Miguel was born, when he'd seemed irritated by Miguel's cries when my son's tummy hurt or he was unable to sleep. Edward had made several dark hints about adoption, or sending the baby back to Claudie and Alejandro. I'd thought Edward's jokes were in poor taste, but I'd let it go, because I owed him so much.

But now—

Edward was no longer even looking at me. He was smiling at Alejandro, utterly confident—like a dog who couldn't wait to test out his slashing claws and snarling teeth, to prove who was the stronger, meaner dog, in the pretext for a brawl of fighting over a bone—me.

Alejandro's dark eyes met mine. For a moment, they held. Something changed in his expression. He seemed to relax slightly. He drew himself up, looking almost amused.

"Yes, Lena is the mother of my child," he drawled. "And because of that I have a claim on her that you never will. But that's not the only claim. I have one deeper even than that." He glanced at me. "We intended to keep it private for a few days more, as a family matter, but we might as well let everyone know, shall we not, *querida?*"

"Um, yes?" I said, as mystified as everyone else.

Still smiling that pleasant smile, Alejandro turned and grabbed a crystal flute and solid silver knife off a waiter's passing tray. For a moment I froze in fear. Even with a butter knife—heck, even with his bare hands—I knew Alejandro could be dangerous. Boxing and mixed martial arts were hobbies in his downtime, the way he kept in shape and worked out the tension from a hard day making billion-dollar deals.

I exhaled when he didn't turn back to attack Edward. In fact, he rather insultingly turned his back on him, striding through the ballroom, to the dais, as the crowds parted like magic. He climbed the steps to the same microphone where he'd given the speech before. Most of the guests, seeing him, immediately fell silent. A few continued to whisper amongst themselves, staring between him and Edward—and me.

Alejandro chimed his knife against the crystal flute, so hard and loud that I feared the delicate glass might break in his hand. The entire ballroom fell so quiet that I could hear my own breath.

"I know this is a business gathering," he said, "but I must beg your indulgence for a moment. I am, after all, amongst friends...." His eyes abruptly focused on me across the crowd. "I have some happy news to announce. My engagement."

No. My face turned red and my body itched in an attack of nervous fear beneath my pale pink ball gown as a thousand people turned to stare at me. The whispering increased, building like the roll of distant thunder.

"Many of you probably wondered if I'd *ever* get married." Alejandro rubbed the back of his dark hair then looked up with a smile that was equal parts charming and sheepish. "I confess I wondered that myself." His low, sexy voice reverberated across the gilded ballroom. "But sometimes fate chooses better for us than we could ever have chosen for ourselves."

No, no, no, I pleaded desperately with my eyes. He smiled.

He lifted his champagne flute toward me. "A toast. To Miss Lena Carlisle. The most beautiful woman on earth, and the mother of my baby son…"

The whispers exploded to a sharp roar.

"…to the future Duchess of Alzacar!"

There were gasps across the crowd, the largest of which was probably mine. But Alejandro continued to hold up his flute, so everyone else did, too. He drank deeply, and a thousand guests drank, too. Toasting to our engagement.

Only two people continued to stare at him blankly.

Edward.

And me.

My body trembled. All I wanted to do was turn and flee through the crowd, to disappear, to never come back. To be free of him—the man who'd once destroyed me. Who could, if z-he tried, so easily do it again—and more, since now our child could be used against me.

But that child also meant, in a very real way, that I was bound to Alejandro for the rest of my life. We both loved Miguel. We both wished to raise him.

Which meant, no matter how fiercely I wished otherwise, and no matter how I'd tried to deny it, I would never be truly free of Alejandro—ever.

Cheers, some supportive, some envious and some by bewildered drunken people who'd missed what all the fuss was about but were happy to cheer anyway, rang across the ballroom, along with a smattering of applause. Alejandro left the dais, where he was stopped by crowds of well-wishers, including the glamorous movie star I'd recognized and two heads of state.

Behind me, Edward seethed with disappointment and fury, "He doesn't own you."

"You're wrong," I whispered. I turned to Edward with tears in my eyes. "He owned me from the moment I became pregnant with his baby."

Edward's face went wild.

"No," he breathed. He started to reach toward my face, then he stiffened as he became aware of all the people watching us, the strangers starting to hover, no doubt awaiting their chance to congratulate me on snagging a billionaire duke into illustrious matrimony. Gorgeous, beautiful women in designer clothes, thin and glossy like Claudie, were already staring at me incredulously, clearly in shock that someone like me could possibly have captured the heart of a man like Alejandro.

The answer was simple. I hadn't.

This was my future. Everything I thought I'd left behind me in London, all the pity and dismissive insults. Except it would be even worse. Being described as a poor relation was practically a compliment, compared with the epithet that strangers would soon use to describe me: *gold digger.*

It would have been different if Alejandro and I had actually loved each other. Thinking of it, my heart ached. If he'd loved me, and I'd loved him, I wouldn't have given two hoots what anyone else thought. But as it was...

"You agreed to marry him?" Edward said incredulously.

"Not exactly." Swallowing over the ache in my throat, I breathed, "It doesn't matter. Now he has proof he's Miguel's father, he'll never let him go. And I will never leave my son. So we might as well be married...."

"Like hell."

Edward grabbed my arm, his eyes like fire. Without warning, he pulled me through the crowd. I had one single image of Alejandro's shocked face across the ballroom, watching us, before I was out the side door and down the hall, pushed into a dark, quiet corner of the empty coatroom.

Edward turned to me, his face contorted by shadows.

"Run away with me," he said urgently.

I drew back in shock. "What?"

"Navaro has no hold on you."

"He's Miguel's father!"

"Share custody of the kid if you must," he said through gritted teeth. His hand gripped my forearm. "But don't throw yourself away on a man who will never deserve you."

"What are you saying?" I tried to pull away my arm, but his grip was tight.

"He terrified you for a year—got you pregnant just to steal your baby—"

"I was wrong—he didn't! It was all Claudie! She's the one who said it, and I believed her."

"So he's innocent? No way," he said grimly. "But even if he is—even if he didn't do that one awful thing, what about the rest?"

"What do you mean?"

"He made you love him, then he *abandoned* you. Don't you remember how gray your face was for months afterward? How your eyes were hollow and you barely spoke? I do."

I swallowed. "I…"

"Where was he when you wanted to give him

everything? When you tried to tell him you were pregnant? He *changed his phone number.* How can you marry him now? How can you forget?"

I flashed hot, then cold. Yes. I remembered.

"And after all that, he gets you back?" Edward pulled me closer, looking down at me in the shadowy cloakroom with a strange light in his eyes. "No. I was there for you. I took care of you. I'm the one who—"

"Get your hands off my woman."

The low voice was ice-cold behind us. With a gasp that must have sounded guilty, I whirled to face him. "Alejandro!"

His eyes were dark with fury as he looked at me. "So this is why you were so reluctant to marry me?"

"No, you—"

"Be silent!"

I winced.

"Don't talk to her that way," Edward said.

Alejandro didn't look away from me. He held his body in a dangerous stillness as he ground out, "You have nothing to do with us, St. Cyr."

Either Edward didn't see the warning, or he didn't care. "Don't I? Who do you think was supporting her this past year? Who held her together after you blew her apart?" Coming closer to Alejandro, he said softly, with a malicious look in his eyes, "Who was at Lena's side at the hospital, when she gave birth to your child? Where were you then, Navaro?"

Alejandro slowly turned to look at him. I saw the hard set of his shoulders, the rapid rise and fall of his breath. I saw his hands tighten at his sides, and knew Edward was about to lose half of his face.

"Stop!" I cried, stepping between them in real fear. "Stop this at once!" I pressed on Edward's chest. "Just go."

He lifted his eyebrows in shock. "You can't honestly choose him over me?"

"Go. And don't come back." I glanced back at Alejandro and knew only the fact that I stood between them kept him from attack. I took a deep breath. "Thank you for everything you did for me, Edward. I'll never forget how you helped me." My jaw hardened. "But it's over."

Edward's face contorted. "You're throwing yourself away on *him?* Just because of some *stupid baby?*"

My sympathy disintegrated.

"That *stupid baby* is my son."

"Dammit, you know I didn't mean…"

But my heart had iced over. Releasing him, I stepped back, closer to Alejandro. "Yes, I choose him. Over you."

"You heard her," Alejandro said roughly. "You have thirty seconds to be out of my building, before security throws you out."

"Sending in your goons, eh?" he sneered. "Can't be bothered to do it yourself?"

"Happy to," Alejandro said grimly, pushing up the sleeves of his tuxedo jacket as he took a step forward, fists raised.

"No!" I grabbed his arm. My hand couldn't even fully wrap around the full extent of the hard, huge biceps beneath his tuxedo. "Please, Alejandro," I whispered. "Don't hurt him. He was good to me, when I had no one else. I never would have survived without him. Neither would Miguel. Please. For my sake."

Jaw taut, Alejandro slowly lowered his fist. "For your sake." His voice was low and cold as he turned to Edward. "Thank you. For protecting what I love."

Love? For a moment I stared at Alejandro, then I realized he was speaking of Miguel.

Edward glared at him. Obviously not realizing

he'd just narrowly escaped death, he sneered, "Go to hell." At the door, he turned back and said, "I'll be back for you, Lena."

Then he was gone. And Alejandro and I were suddenly alone in the cloakroom. But my relief was short-lived.

"No wonder he loaned you his house," he said. "No wonder he protected you. He sees you as his. Why does he believe that?"

I whirled to face him. The cold fury in his eyes was like a wave. But there was something else there, too. Hurt.

"He tried to kiss me last week," I admitted in a low voice, then shook my head. "But I just gave a shocked laugh and he left. Whatever he might have hoped, all he ever was to me was a friend—"

"*Friend*," he said scornfully. "You knew what he wanted."

I shook my head fiercely. "Not until last week, I never—"

"Then you were willfully blind. He's in love with you."

"You're wrong there." Shivering, I crossed my bare arms over my pink strapless ball gown. "If he'd really loved me, he would have loved Miguel, too. But he was always getting annoyed about him. Suggesting things…like I should send him away, farm him out for adoption…"

Alejandro's eyes darkened. "And you were willing to call him a friend? To let him near our son?"

I wanted to lash back at him. To tell him he was being unreasonable, or that I hadn't had a choice. Instead, I said the only thing that mattered. The only thing that was true.

"I'm sorry," I said in a low voice. "I was wrong."

He'd been opening his mouth to say more, no doubt cutting, angry accusations. But my humble, simple words cut him off at the knees. For a long moment, he stared at me in the shadowy cloakroom. Down the hall, we could distantly hear music playing, people laughing. Then he turned away, clawing back his dark hair.

"*Bien.* I wasn't exactly perfect, either," he muttered. Lifting his head, he glared at me. "But you're never to see him again. Or let him near Miguel."

"Fine," I said.

"Fine?"

"He stopped being my friend the moment he called my baby 'it.'"

"So," he said with a casual tone that belied

the tension in his shoulders, "did you let him kiss you?"

I gaped at him. "Oh—for heaven's sake!" I stomped my foot against the plush carpet. "I'm not going to say it again!"

"I found the two of you here, talking..."

"And I just saw you talking to an actress in the ballroom. I didn't accuse you of making out! He made a pass at me last week. I refused. End of story."

"Once we are married..."

My cheeks went hot. "Married!" I stared at him, shocked. "Who said anything about marriage?"

Now Alejandro was the one to look shocked.

"I just asked you to marry me!"

"*Asked?*" My voice was acid. "When you asked, I said no. Tonight, you just *announced* it! In front of everyone! You may have asked—I never said yes!"

"We are going to be wed. Accept it."

"I will accept *an engagement,*" I retorted. "I will accept that we need to live in the same town, perhaps even the same house, for our son. A public front, a pretense for Miguel's sake, to make it appear we are actually a couple—that he wasn't just some *mistake!* But nothing more. There's no way I'm actually going to *marry* you. Do you think I would ever give you my body again? Or my heart?"

"I told you," he ground out. "I'm not asking for your heart."

"Then you can forget anything else—I won't give you my body, or take your name! I owe you respect as Miguel's father, but that's it," I said through gritted teeth. "Whatever you might believe, you don't own me, any more than Edward did!"

"I'm not Edward. I'm the father of your child." He grabbed my wrist, looking down at me. "I'm the man you will wed. I don't need your heart. But your body, at least, will be mine."

"No!" But even as I gasped with fury, heat flashed from his possessive grip on my wrist. Electricity crackled up my arm, to my throat, to my lips, to my breasts, down, down, down to my core. Pushing me back roughly against the coats, he looked down at me in the shadows.

"Did you really think," he said softly, "once I found you, I would ever let you go? I gave you up once for the sake of a promise. I gave you up to *do the right thing*. But fate has thrown you back into my arms. Now you will be entirely mine—"

Lowering his head, Alejandro kissed me fiercely, his lips hot and hard against mine, plundering, demanding. I tried to resist. I couldn't let myself feel—I couldn't—

Then I melted as the banked embers inside me, beneath the cold ash of the past lonely year, roared to a blazing fire. My body shuddered beneath his ruthless, almost violent embrace, and I wrapped my arms tightly around him, holding him to me, lost in the sweet forbidden ecstasy of surrender.

CHAPTER FIVE

HIS LIPS SAVAGED MINE, his tongue hot and salty and sweet. I clutched his shoulders, desperate to sate my desire. I'd hungered for him every night, even when I hated him, against all reason, against my will.

Alejandro's hands ran along my bare arms then moved to the tangle in my hair, tilting my chin so he could plunder my mouth more deeply. Long tendrils of hair had pulled free from my chignon. I felt them brush against my naked shoulders as his hard, muscular body strained against me, towering over mine, overpowering me. But it wasn't enough. Not nearly enough…

His hot kisses moved slowly down my neck, as he murmured husky endearments in Spanish against my skin. My head fell back against the wall of coats, and I closed my eyes, feeling tight and dizzy. He nuzzled my bare skin over the neckline of my gown. His hands cupped my breasts straining against the pink silk of the bodice.

So sweet. So hot. My breath came at a gasp, and as my eyelids flickered, the world seemed to spin in whirling patterns of shadows and light, echoes of past love and longing. For over a year I'd longed for him. For all my life, I'd longed for this. And it was even better than I remembered, a powerful drug beyond imagining. Wrapped in his embrace, I forgot myself, forgot my own name, and knew only that I had to have him or die....

A low deliberate cough came behind us. Startled, I turned my head, and Alejandro straightened. The Bulgarian ambassador stood at the cloakroom door, with his wife draped in pearls behind him.

"Excuse us," he said gravely, and stepping forward, he took a black fur coat off the hanger behind us.

I heard his wife titter as they left, "See, Vasil? I told you it was a love match!"

"Poor devil deserves some pleasure, at least," the man's reply echoed back to us, "after the grasping creature tricked him into marriage with a pregnancy."

Shamefaced, I looked up at Alejandro. The air in the cloakroom suddenly felt thin and cold.

"Let me go," I said.

His hold on me only tightened. "Who cares what they say?"

"I care," I whispered.

"Bull," he cut me off ruthlessly. "You're too strong to be ruled by gossip." His hands moved slowly down the bare skin of my upper back, and I shivered, fighting my own desire. "It's this you're afraid of. This." He stroked my arms to my breast, then abruptly pulled me up to stand, hard against his body. "This is all that matters...."

"It's not," I choked out. "There's love. And trust...."

"Love for our son. And trust for your husband. Your partner."

For a second, I trembled. I did want those things. A real home. I'd already accepted that we would need to live in the same town, or better yet, the same house. Why not accept a partnership? We could share a life, a son, even a bed. Would it be enough, without romantic love? Could I live without that? Could I?

For Miguel's sake?

"Maybe I could accept a marriage without love," I said in a small voice. I took a deep breath and raised my gaze to his. "But there is no partnership without trust. Can you promise you've never lied to me? And that you never will?"

I watched as the brief triumph in his eyes went out. "No."

My lips parted in a silent gasp. I hadn't expected that. My heart twisted as I thought how, with just a few hot kisses and the dream of giving Miguel a real home and family, I'd been perilously close to giving up my dreams.

"Well, which is it, Alejandro?" I choked out. "Did you lie to me in the past? Or will you lie to me in the future?"

His jawline tightened. For a moment, his face seemed tortured. Then, as I'd seen happen before, his expression shuttered, becoming expressionless, leaving me to wonder if I'd imagined the whole thing. "Take your pick."

I stiffened. Hating him—no. Hating *myself* for letting him kiss me. Letting him? All he'd had to do was touch me and I'd flung myself into his kiss with the hunger of a starving woman at a piece of bread. "What have you lied to me about?"

"You expect me to tell you the truth about that?"

"Other women?"

He glared at me. "I told you. I believe in honor. Fidelity. No. My lie is about—something else."

"What?"

"Me," he ground out through gritted teeth. "Only me."

Which didn't tell me anything at all! "Fine. Whatever." I glared at him. "You shouldn't have kissed me."

He relaxed imperceptibly now that we were no longer talking about his secrets.

"This isn't the place," he agreed.

"I didn't just mean the cloakroom. I mean anywhere."

"I can think of many places I'd like to kiss you."

"Too bad." My cheeks flamed, but I wouldn't let him distract me. "Take your kisses, and your lies, somewhere else."

"A marriage in name only?" He sounded almost amused. "Do you really think that will work?"

"Since I can't even trust you, let alone love you, there will be no marriage of any kind," I snapped. "And if you keep asking, even our engagement will be remarkably short."

"Why are you trying to fight me, when it's so obvious that you will give in?" he said. "You want to raise Miguel. So do I. What do you expect to do—live next door? In my stable?"

"Better that than your bed."

His dark eyes glittered. "That wasn't how you kissed me."

Heat pulsed through me. I could hardly deny it. I looked away. "Sex is different for women. It involves love!"

He snorted. "Right."

"Or at least caring and trust!" I cried, stung.

"Who is speaking in generalities now?" he said harshly. A cynical light rose in his eyes. "Many women have sex with strangers. Just—as you said—as many women prefer to drink their coffee black, without the niceties of sugar and cream!"

My cheeks flushed. "Fine for them, but—"

"Lust is just an appetite, a craving, such as one might have for *ensaladilla rusa*. No one says that you must be deeply committed to the mayonnaise in order to enjoy the taste of the potato salad!"

I lifted my chin. "Go seduce one of those salad women, then! I don't want you in my bed, I don't want you as my husband and I just regret I'm stuck with you as Miguel's father!"

"Enough." His voice was deadly cold. "You have made enough of a fool of me, making me beg— for the truth about Miguel, for the DNA test, for access to him. I even had to beg you to keep your promise to come to Spain. There will be no more begging, at least—" his eyes glittered "—no more begging from me."

Alejandro had begged me for stuff? I must have missed that. "I never—"

"You will marry me. Tonight."

"Don't be ridiculous!"

"Right now. Choose." His expression had hardened. "A priest. Or a lawyer."

"Are you threatening me?"

"Call it what you want."

I licked my lips, then tried, "Edward would help me. He has money and power to match even yours...."

"Ah." Alejandro came closer, softly tucking back a long tendril of hair that had escaped when he'd crushed me a few moments ago in his passionate embrace. "I wondered how long it would be before Mr. St. Cyr's name made an appearance. That was even quicker than I expected."

My cheeks went hot, but I lifted my chin. "He would still help me if I asked."

"Oh, I'm sure he would," he said softly. "But are you willing to accept the cost of his help?"

I swallowed.

"And the price to Miguel. Think of it." He tilted his head. "A custody war, when each side has infinite resources to pay lawyers for years, decades, to come." He gave a brief, humorless smile. "Miguel's first words after *mamá* and *papá* might be *restraining order*."

I sucked in my breath.

"And the scandal… The press will have a field day." Pressing his advantage, he stroked my cheek almost tenderly. "Miguel will grow so accustomed to paparazzi he'll start to think of them as members of his family. With good reason, for he'll see them more frequently than he sees either of us." He dropped his hand. His voice became harsh. "Is that really what you want?"

"Why are you doing this, Alejandro?" I choked out.

"I won't risk having Edward St. Cyr as my son's future stepfather."

I shook my head. "It will never happen!"

"I'm supposed to believe that? A few minutes ago, you promised you'd never see him again. Now you're threatening to use his wealth and power in a custody battle against me."

He looked at me with scorn, and I didn't blame him. I wiped my eyes. "You're right. I shouldn't have done that—but you're forcing my back against the wall! I have no choice!"

"Neither do I." His sensual lips curved downward. "You think you can control him. You cannot. He's selfish. Ruthless. Dangerous."

I flashed him a glare full of hate. "Are you talking about him," I said bitterly, "or yourself?"

"Yes, I could be dangerous," he said softly. "If anyone tried to hurt someone I cared about. I would die—or kill—to protect someone I loved."

"But you don't love anyone!"

"You're wrong." His voice was low. His lips pressed together in a thin line. "So will it be marriage between us—or war?"

"I hate you!"

"Is that your final answer?"

Tears of hopeless rage filled my eyes, but I'd told Edward the truth. Alejandro had owned me from the moment I'd become pregnant with his child. I would give anything, sacrifice any part of myself, for my son. My heart. My dreams. My soul. What were those, compared with Miguel's heart, his dreams, his soul?

My baby would not spend his childhood in and out of divorce courts, surrounded by pushy paparazzi, bewildered by the internecine battles of his parents. Instead, he would be safe and warm and surrounded by love. He would be happy.

It was all I had to cling to. All I had to live for. My shoulders fell.

"No," I whispered. "You win. I will marry you."

"Now."

"Fine! I hate you!"

He looked down at me, his expression sardonic. "Hate me, then. At least that I can believe. Far more than your so-called *love*. But you will be my wife. In every way."

Yanking me into his arms, he kissed me, hard. But this time, there was nothing of tenderness, or even passion. Just a ruthless act of possession, showing me he owned me, a savage kiss hard enough to bruise.

Pulling me out of the cloakroom and outside into the warm Spanish night, he called for his driver. The paparazzi were long gone, and the street was quiet, even lonely.

Alejandro took me to the house of a local official, where with a quiet word a certificate of permission to marry was produced in record time. Then to a priest, in a large, empty church, so old and full of shadows it seemed half-haunted with the lost dreams of the dead.

And so Alejandro and I were wed, in that wan, barren church, with only flickers of candlelight and ghostly moonlight from the upper windows lighting the cold, pale marble. My pink ball gown of silk and embroidered flowers, which once seemed so beautiful, now hung on me like a shroud.

There was no wedding dress. No cake. No flowers. And no one, except the priest and his assistant called as witness, to wish us happiness.

Which was just as well, because as I looked at the savage face of my new husband as we left the church into the dark of night, I knew happiness was the one thing we'd never have.

Alejandro looked across the front seat of the car. "You're going to have to talk to me at some point."

I looked out the window at the passing scenery as we drove south into Andalucía. "No, I don't, actually."

"So you intend to ignore me forever?" he said drily.

I shrugged, still not looking at him. "Lots of married couples stop talking eventually. We might as well start now."

We'd been alone in the car together for hours, but it felt like days. Alejandro was driving the expensive sports sedan, with Miguel in the baby seat behind us, cooing and batting at plush dangling toys. Three bodyguards and his usual driver were in the SUV following us. "I want some private time with my new bride," Alejandro had told them with a wink, and they'd grinned.

But the reason he'd desired privacy wasn't exactly the usual one for newlyweds. I'd given Alejandro the silent treatment since our ghastly wedding ceremony last night. Seething. It wasn't natural for me to bite my tongue. I think he was waiting for me to explode.

He'd gotten me home by midnight as promised. The instant we returned to his Madrid penthouse I'd stalked into the bedroom where my baby slept, and though I couldn't slam the door—too noisy—I'd locked it solidly behind me. Very childish, but I'd been afraid that once Mrs. Gutierrez left, he might demand his rights of the wedding night. Pulling on flannel pajamas, I'd stared at the door, just daring him to try.

But he hadn't. About three in the morning, feeling foolish, I'd unlocked the door. But he never came, not even to apologize for his brutish behavior. There was no way I would have let him seduce me...but my nose was slightly out of joint that he hadn't even bothered to try. Our marriage was only a few hours old, and he was already ignoring me?

I didn't see him until this morning, when he was coming out of the guest bathroom next door, looking well rested and obviously straight out of the shower. His dark hair was wet, a low-slung towel wrapped around his bare hips and another towel hanging over his broad, naked shoulders.

I'd stopped flat in the hallway, unable to look away from the muscular planes of his bare chest, laced with dark hair, or the powerful lines of his body, to the slim hips barely covered by the clinging white terry cloth.

Alejandro had greeted me with a sensual smile. "Good morning, *querida,*" he'd purred, then lifting a wicked eyebrow as if he already knew the answer, he'd inquired, "I trust you slept well?"

But I was starting to get my revenge. His lips were now set in an annoyed line as he kept his eyes on the road, pressing on the gas of his very expensive, very fast sedan. "We are husband and wife now, Lena. You must accept that."

"Oh, I do," I assured him. "But we're a husband and wife who happen to hate each other. So perhaps just not talking is best."

Alejandro exhaled in irritation, his hands tightening on the steering wheel. I turned away, staring out wistfully at the scenery of Spain flying past us. In any other circumstance I would have been in awe at the magnificent view. The farmland and soft hills of central Spain were turning to a drier landscape. Lovely thick bushes of pink and white oleander flowers separated the highway, a vivid, wild, unexpected beauty, much like Spain itself.

Oleander. I shivered a little. So beautiful to the eyes. But so poisonous to the heart.

Just like Alejandro, I thought. I wouldn't let him in. Husband or not, I'd never let him close to me. In any way.

We'd stopped only once since we left Madrid, to feed and change the baby, and to put gas in both cars. Alejandro offered to take a small detour and stop for lunch in Córdoba, to show me the famous cathedral that had once been a Great Mosque. But I'd refused. I didn't want him doing me any favors. Though later I regretted it, because I heard a lot about the famous Mezquita.

As the car flew south, turning on a new road, I blinked in the bright sun flooding the windows. After weeks of rain in San Miguel, and London's drizzle and overcast skies, the Spanish sun had come as advertised, with a wide blue horizon that held not a single cloud. The arid landscape suddenly reminded me of Mexico. Which reminded me of the freedom and independence I'd had so briefly.

And Edward.

I'll be back for you, Lena.

"Stop it," Alejandro growled.

I nearly jumped in the smooth leather seat. "What?"

"I can hear you. Thinking about him."

"You can hear me thinking?"

"Stop," he said quietly, giving me a hard sideways glance. "Or I will make you stop."

"*Make* me—" I snorted derisively, then I looked at him, remembering his last ruthless kiss in the cloakroom. And the one before it, which had been even more dangerous. I remembered how it had felt, surrendering to his embrace, how it had made my whole body tremble with need.

"You're such a jerk," I muttered, folding my arms mutinously. "My thoughts are my own."

"Not if they are of a man like St. Cyr. Thoughts lead to actions."

"I told you, I don't even like him anymore!"

He snorted. "And that is supposed to inspire trust? You've made it plain you did not wish to marry me. Perhaps you're wishing now you took the other choice."

I looked at him. "What other choice?"

"A war between us," he said grimly. He was staring forward at the road, his jaw tight. "St. Cyr would be eager to help you with that."

My arms unfolded. "No." I frowned. "I don't want war. I'd never deliberately hurt you, Alejandro. Not now."

"Really," he said in clear disbelief.

"Hurting you would hurt Miguel." I looked out the window and said softly, "We both love him. I realized the truth last night, even before your marriage ultimatum—neither of us wants to be apart from him." Blinking fast, I faced him. "You're right. We're married now. So let's make the best of it."

"Do you mean it?" he said evenly. I nodded.

"Let's make sure Miguel has a wonderful childhood and a real home, where he'll always feel safe and warm and loved."

His hands seemed to relax a little around the steering wheel. He looked at me. There was something strange in his eyes, something almost like— yearning—that made my heart twist.

"If it's really true you'd never deliberately hurt

me..." He seemed to be speaking to himself. "I wish I could..."

"What?"

He shook his head, and his jaw went hard. "Nothing."

What had he been about to say? I looked down, blinking as my eyes burned. Telling myself I shouldn't care. Willing myself *not* to care.

My lie is about something else.

What?

I remembered the stark look in his eyes. *Me. Only me.*

Stop it, I told my heart fiercely. *Don't get sucked in! Keep your distance!*

Silently, Alejandro stared forward at the road. For long minutes, the only sound was Miguel cooing to himself in the backseat, chortling triumphantly as he grasped a soft toy hanging from the top of his baby seat, and making it squeak. I smiled back at my son. He was the reason. The only reason.

"I'm glad you feel that way. The truth is I don't want to hurt you, either." Alejandro tightened his hands on the steering wheel. He glanced at me out of the corner of his eye. "Our son is what matters. We'll focus on him. I'll never leave you or

Miguel. Together we'll make sure our son is always well cared for."

Our eyes locked, and an ache lifted to my throat. Turning away, I tried to block the emotion out with a laugh. "Miguel will be a duke someday. That's crazy, isn't it?"

Alejandro turned his eyes back to the road.

"Sí," he said grimly. "Crazy."

I'd been trying to lighten the mood. But his voice sounded darker than ever. "Did I say something wrong?"

"No. You are correct. Miguel will be Duque de Alzacar." I frowned. But before I could figure out what lay behind the odd tension in his voice, he turned to me. "So you forgive me for forcing you to marry me against your will?"

I exhaled.

"It's a very complicated question."

"No. It is not."

Something broke inside me. And words came pouring out.

"You think I was silly and selfish to want to marry for love. But for the past ten years, that dream was all I've held on to." I looked at my hands in my lap. "Ever since I was fourteen years old, I've felt so alone. So unwanted. But then, last year, when I met you…" I lifted agonized eyes to his. "All my dreams seemed to be coming true. It was as if…I'd gone back in time. To the world I once knew. The one filled with love. The world where I was good enough. Wanted. Even cherished."

Alejandro's expression darkened. "Lena…"

"Then you abandoned me," I whispered. "You told me you didn't love me, that you never would." I looked at him. "But I still married you yesterday, Alejandro, knowing that. Knowing you've lied to me in the past and will lie in the future. I married you knowing that the loneliness I tried to leave behind me in London will now follow me for the rest of my life. Only now, instead of being a poor relation, I'm the gold digger who got pregnant to ensnare a rich duke. And everyone will say, weren't you so good and noble to marry me? Wasn't it an amazing sacrifice for you to make me your wife? How generous of you! How kind!"

He glowered. "No one will say that."

I cut him off with a low laugh. "*Everyone* will. And I know there will be days when I'll feel that marrying you was the biggest mistake of my life." I drew a deep, shuddering breath, then met his gaze. "And yet I can't regret it," I whispered. "Because it will make Miguel's life better to have you in his life. Every single day. He will know you. Really know you."

"I wish he could." Alejandro stared at me. His dark eyes were liquid and deep. "I wish I could tell you…"

I held my breath. "Yes?"

His face suddenly turned cold, like a statue. He looked away. "Forget it."

I exhaled, wishing I hadn't said so much.

He drove the car off the main road, then took a smaller one, then turned on a private lane that was smaller still, nothing but a ribbon twisting across the broad-swept lands. Alejandro stopped briefly at a tall iron gate, then entered a code into the electronic keypad. We proceeded inside the estate, which looked so endless and wide, I wondered how anyone had wrapped a fence around it, and if the fence was visible from space, like the Great Wall of China.

Then I saw the castle, high on a distant hill, and I sucked in my breath. It was like a fairy-tale castle, rising with ramparts of stone and turrets stretching into the sky.

"Is that…?" I breathed.

"*Sí,*" Alejandro said quietly. "My home. The

Castillo de Rohares. The home of the Dukes of Alzacar for four hundred years."

It took another fifteen minutes to climb the hill, past the groves of olive trees and orange trees. When we reached the castle at last, past the ramparts into a courtyard surrounding a stone fountain, he stopped the car at the grand entrance on the circular driveway. He turned off the engine, and I could hear the bodyguards climbing out of the SUV behind us, talking noisily about lunch, slamming doors. But as I started to turn for the passenger-side door, Alejandro grabbed my wrist. I turned to face him, and he dropped my arm.

"I am sorry I hurt you, Lena. When I left you last summer, when I refused to return any of your phone calls—I did that for good reason. At least—" his jaw tightened "—it seemed like good reason."

"No, I get it," I said. "You didn't want me to love you."

"No. That's not it at all." He lifted his dark eyes to mine. "I didn't leave because you loved me. I left because I was falling in love with you."

CHAPTER SIX

I STARED AT him in shock.

"What?" I breathed.

A hard knock banged against the car window behind me, making me jump. Turning my head, I saw a plump smiling woman, standing on the driveway outside, dressed in an apron and holding a spoon. She waved at us merrily. I saw the bodyguards greeting her with obvious affection as they went into the grand stone entrance of the castle.

"Another housekeeper?" I said faintly.

"My grandmother," he said.

"Your—" I whirled to face him, but he had already opened his door and was getting out of the car, gently lifting Miguel out of his baby seat. Nervously, I got out of the car, too, wondering what the dowager Duchess of Alzacar would make of me.

"Come in, come in," she said to the bodyguards, shooing them inside. She kept switching from

English to Spanish as if she couldn't quite make up her mind. "Knowing Alejandro, I'm sure you didn't stop for any lunch, so everything is ready if you'll just go straight to the banqueting hall…"

"Abuela," Alejandro said, smiling, "I'd like you to meet my son. His name is Miguel."

"Miguel?" she gasped, looking from him to Alejandro.

He blinked with a slight frown, shaking his head. "And this is my new wife. Lena."

"I'm so happy to meet you." Smoothing one hand over her apron, she turned to me with a warm smile, lifting the wooden spoon high, like a benign domestic fairy about to grant a really good wish. "And your sweet baby! I can hardly wait to…" Her eyes suddenly narrowed. "Your new what?"

Coming over to me, Alejandro put his free arm around my shoulders. "My wife."

She lowered her spoon and looked me over, from my long hair to my soft white blouse with the Peter Pan collar, to my slim-cut jeans and ballet flats. I braced myself for criticism.

Instead, she beamed at me, spreading her arms wide.

"Oh, my dear," she cried, "welcome to the family. Welcome to your new home!"

And she threw her arms around me in a big, fierce, welcoming hug.

Shocked, I stiffened. Then I patted her awkwardly on the back.

"But I'm being silly," she said, drawing back, wiping her eyes with her brightly colored apron. "My name is Maurine. But please call me Abuela, if you like, as Alejandro does. Or Grandma. Or Nana. Whatever. I'm just so happy you're here!"

"Thank you," I said, unsure how to handle such immediate warmth and kindness.

"But you—" she whirled on her grandson with a scowl "—you should have known better than to elope!"

Alejandro looked abashed. It was a funny, boyish expression on his masculine face. "We would have waited and had a proper wedding," he said, rubbing his neck sheepishly, "but Abuela, it happened so quickly…."

"Huh. Don't think you're getting off that easy. We'll talk about it later. Now—" her plump face softened as her eyes lit up "—let me hold that baby."

Ten minutes later, Maurine was giving me a speed tour of the castle, on the way to the dining hall. "The foundations of Rohares date from the times of the sultan," she said happily. "But most of the building dates from the early seventeenth century. It was bombed in the war, then when we came back we had no money and it fell into disrepair." She looked sad, then brightened, smiling up at her grandson. "But Alejandro made his fortune in Madrid, then restored every part of it, made Rohares better than it had ever been before! And here's where we'll have lunch...."

I stopped in the huge doorway of an enormous dining hall that looked as if it came from the late Renaissance, complete with soaring frescoed ceilings, suits of armor beside the ancient tapestries and a stone fireplace tall enough to fit a person inside. And at the center of the huge, gymnasium-size room, there was a long wooden dining table, large enough to seat forty or fifty people, and groaning beneath the weight of the luncheon spread, flower arrangements, and place settings carefully designed with fine china and the brightest decor.

My mouth dropped as I stared at it.

"Cold and drafty, *si?*" Alejandro said smugly, grabbing a marinated green olive and piece of cheese off the platter on the table. "Just as you said."

"I've never seen anything like this," I breathed. "And the food…"

He gave a low chuckle. "Abuela believes food is love."

"I can see that," I said faintly, staring up at his face.

I left because I was falling in love with you.

My knees were still weak at what he'd said in the car. It was so far from everything I'd ever imagined, I couldn't believe I'd heard him right. "Alejandro…"

"Abuela can be bossy about it, but she loves nothing more than taking care of people, along with her garden and home." He grinned, shaking his head ruefully. "She now has an unlimited budget, a clear schedule—now she's given up her charity work—and infinite time. When it comes to the domestic arts, she is unstoppable."

"Amazing." I looked at him hesitantly. "But Alejandro…"

"Yes?"

"Did you mean what you said?"

His dark eyes met mine. He knew what I was talking about. "Don't be afraid. As you said—much has changed in this past year."

I hadn't realized I'd been holding my breath,

but at that, I exhaled, like air fizzing out of a tire. "You're right," I said, keeping my voice steady. "Everything is different now."

"The past is past. Now we are partners, parents to our son."

"Exactly." I looked away. The bodyguards, apparently accustomed to being fed lunch like this by the dowager duchess, were already at the table, filling their plates and murmuring their appreciation.

Maurine suddenly reappeared in the solid-oak doorway, holding Miguel with one hand, a small card in the other. Going to the table, she snatched a card off a place setting, then replaced it with the new card. Turning back, she patted the chair, beaming at me. "You're to sit here, dear."

"Oh. Thank you, Maurine."

Smiling, she looked at Miguel in her arms, and started another peekaboo game. She'd been lost in baby joy from the instant she'd picked him up in her arms, and the love appeared to be mutual. I watched, smiling, as Maurine hid her face with her hand, before revealing it so Miguel could reach out to bat her nose triumphantly, leaving them both in hopeless squeals of laughter. Alejandro watched them, too.

"Thank you," he said quietly.

"For what?"

His dark eyes met mine. "For coming to Spain like you promised."

"Oh." My cheeks flooded with shame to remember how I'd initially refused. "It's, um, nothing."

He turned away, watching his grandmother play with his son. "It's everything to me."

My blush deepened, then I sighed. "I was wrong to fight it," I admitted.

"You? Wrong?" Alejandro shook his head. "Impossible."

I scowled at his teasing tone. "Yes, wrong. I'm woman enough to admit it. After all, Maurine is Miguel's family, too." I looked around the huge banqueting hall, filled with antiques that seemed hundreds of years old. I had to crane my head back to see the wood-timbered ceiling, with its faded paintings of the ducal coat of arms. "And this is his legacy," I said softly. "This will all belong to him someday...."

Alejandro was no longer smiling.

"Yes," he said. "It will."

For some reason I didn't understand, the lightness of the mood had fled. I frowned.

He abruptly held out his arm. "Let's have lunch, shall we?"

Even through his long-sleeved shirt, I could feel the warmth of his arm. The strength of it. From the end of the long table, I saw the bodyguards looking at us, saw one of them nudge the other with a sly grin. To outward appearance, we must have looked like goofy-in-love newlyweds.

Alejandro pulled out the chair Maurine had chosen for me, waited, then after I sat down, he pushed it in and sat beside me.

Looking down at the table, I saw three different plates of different sizes stacked on top of each other in alternating colors. At the top of the place setting, there was a homemade paper flower of red-and-purple tissue paper, very similar to the paper flowers my mother had made for me when I was young. Beside it was a card that held a small hand-written name, with elegant black-ink calligraphy.

The Duchess of Alzacar
my darling new granddaughter

Looking at it, a lump rose in my throat. "Look what she wrote."

Alejandro looked at the card, and smiled. "Yes."

"She's already accepted me in the family. Just like that?"

"Just like that." He made me a plate with a little of everything, and poured me a glass of sparkling water, then red wine.

"Wine for lunch?" I said doubtfully.

"It's from my vineyard by the coast. You should try it."

"All right," I sighed. I took a sip, then said in amazement, "It's delicious."

"You sound surprised."

"Is there anything you're not good at?" I said a little sulkily. He smiled.

Then the smile fled from his handsome face. His dark eyes turned hollow, even bleak.

"Keeping promises," he said.

The blow was so sudden and unexpected that it felt like an anvil hitting the softest part of my belly. The moment I'd let my defenses down, he'd spoken with such unprovoked cruelty it took my breath away. Reminding me.

Did you lie to me in the past? Or will you lie to me in the future?

Take your pick.

"Oh," I breathed, dropping my fork with a

clang against the twenty-four-karat-gold-rimmed china plate.

He'd done me a favor reminding me, I told myself savagely. I couldn't start believing the pretense. I couldn't start thinking we were actually a family. That we were actually in love. I couldn't surrender!

And yet…

"Are you enjoying yourself, dear?" I looked up to see Maurine smiling down at me from the other side of the table, with chubby Miguel still smiling in her arms. "I hope you see something you like!"

"I do," I replied automatically, then realized to my horror that the exact moment I'd spoken the words I'd been looking at Alejandro. Quickly, I looked down at my plate. "What's this?" I asked, looking at one of the dishes, some kind of meat with leeks and carrots.

"*Pato a la Sevillana,* a specialty of the area. Slow-cooked duck roasted in sherry and vegetables."

I took a bite. It was delicious. "And this?"

"*Rabo de toro.* Another classic dish of Andalucía. Vegetables, slowly braised with sherry and bay leaf."

Bull's tail? I tasted it. Not bad. I tried the fresh

papayas and mangoes, the *albóndigas,* the fried-potato-and-ham *croquetas.* I smiled. *"Delicioso!"*

"Muy bien," Maurine sighed happily, then turned on her grandson, tossing her chic, white hair. "Though *you* don't deserve lunch. I should let you get fast food at a drive-through in Seville!" She hitched her great-grandbaby higher on her hip against her pinafore apron. "I cannot believe you got married without inviting me to the wedding! My only family! After I waited thirty-five years to see you get married! After the way you used to make me bite my nails over those wretched skinny, self-centered women you used to cavort with!"

"At least I didn't marry one of them, eh, Abuela? Do I not get credit for that?"

"Yes," she sighed. "On that, you did well."

The two of them smiled at each other, and I had the sudden image of what it must have been like for him to be raised by Maurine in this enormous castle. Alejandro had lost his parents even younger than I'd lost mine. My father had died of a stroke, my mother six months later of illness. But Alejandro had lost both parents in a car crash when he was only twelve. He'd also lost his best friend, Miguel, whom he'd thought of as a brother, and even their housekeeper.

My smile suddenly faltered. All this time, I'd moaned and whimpered so much about my own difficult childhood. But Alejandro had barely hinted aloud about his. A very masculine reticence, but enough to make me writhe with shame. No wonder Alejandro had been so determined that our Miguel, his only child, should come back to Spain, his home, and meet his grandmother, his only family, who'd raised him and loved him.

Even though she didn't seem to be one hundred percent loving him right now.

"But still." His grandmother's chin was wobbling. "All I asked was that you let me attend the wedding. It was my one and only chance to see you get married and I…"

"It was the worst wedding ever," I heard myself blurt out.

Both of them turned to face me. She looked amazed. He looked faintly strangled, as if he were afraid of what I might say next.

"It was just the two of us—" I shook my head "—along with the priest and some stranger as witness. There was no cake. No flowers. You didn't miss anything, Maurine!"

"Call me Abuela, dear," she said faintly. Her gaze softened as she looked at me. Whatever anger she was now lavishing on Alejandro clearly did not extend to me. She blinked with a frown, tilting her head. "You didn't have any flowers? Not one?"

"It's not entirely his fault," I said apologetically. "We felt we should get married immediately, without too much fuss, because of…" I glanced at our baby in her arms.

"Ah." A look of understanding filled her eyes. "Yes, of course."

"The legal part is done, but Alejandro was just saying on the drive that he wished we could have a reception, a party of some kind, to introduce me to his neighbors and friends. I mean, he did tell a few people in Madrid that we were engaged—" I looked at Alejandro beneath my lashes "—but that's not the same as celebrating with neighbors and family."

"No, it's not," she said thoughtfully.

Taking a bite of juicy ripe papaya, I sighed. "But we just don't know what to do. I mean, Alejandro is so busy with his company, and of course I have my hands full with Miguel. I wouldn't have a clue how to organize a party anyway, not a big one. So we were thinking we could maybe hire a party planner, maybe from Madrid...."

"A *party planner!*" Maurine gasped indignantly. "My new granddaughter—and my great-grandson, this little angel—introduced to all my neighbors and friends with some dreary, chic party arranged by a paid *Madrileño!*" She put a dramatic hand over her fulsome chest. "I would turn over in my grave!"

Alejandro's eyes met mine. His lips quirked as he said, "But Abuela, you're not dead."

"You're right, I'm not," she snapped. "Which is why *I* will be planning your wedding reception. Oh, there's no time to waste." Turning away with Miguel still in her arms, she hurried from the dining hall, calling, "María! Carmen! Josefa! Hurry! We have a new project—the most important party I've ever done!"

I turned back to my lunch, only to find Alejandro looking at me. He said in a low voice, "Why did you do that?"

The intense way he was looking at me made me feel nervous and fluttery inside. "Do what?"

"You could have told her the real reason for our quick marriage. That I forced you to marry me, against your will. That I threatened a custody battle."

"Oh." Awkwardly, I looked back at my plate. I took another bite of the *Pato a la Sevillana.* He just waited. Finally, I said in a small voice, "I didn't want to tell her that."

Alejandro came closer, the hard edges of his jaw and cheekbones leaving shadows across his face. "Why?"

My cheeks felt hot. I couldn't meet his eyes.

"Were you trying to protect her?" He was so close now that I could almost feel the heat through his black tailored shirt. My gaze remained down, resting on his shirt just below his ribcage. Just below his heart. His voice was so quiet I could barely hear as he said, "Or were you trying to protect me?"

"You," I whispered.

The only noise in the cavernous dining hall was the distant murmured conversation of the bodyguards sitting at the far end of the table, the clink of silverware against china, the thunk of wineglasses against the wood.

Alejandro leaned forward, his elbow against the long oak table, bringing his face very close to mine. It was almost painful to be that close to so much masculine beauty. Unwillingly, my eyes traced the hard slant of his cheekbones, the rough edge of his jawline. His darkly intent eyes.

And his sensual mouth. That most of all. I watched, unable to look away, as his lips moved to shape a single word.

"Why?"

I swallowed, sweeping my hand to indicate the elaborate decorations and luncheon spread down the long table.

"She loves you. And you love her." I shook my head and blurted out, "All this time I've been moaning about my family in London. I feel so stupid for complaining about my childhood—while all the time, you yourself—"

He put his hand on my cheek. "It doesn't matter now."

Our eyes locked. I caught my breath, feeling the warmth of his fingertips brushing my skin. Feeling how much, deep inside, I wanted him to touch me. On my cheek. Down my neck. Everywhere. Unwillingly, I licked my lips.

But I couldn't give in. I couldn't surrender. If I ever gave him my body, as I'd done the year before, my heart would follow. And I didn't think my shattered heart could survive when he betrayed me as he inevitably would—hadn't he told me as much himself?

Is there anything you're not good at?

Keeping promises.

I pulled back, suddenly desperate to get away from the dangerous energy sizzling between us.

"You love each other. You're a family." My voice trembled, betraying me. "I want you to be happy."

He suddenly leaned forward, his eyes dark.

"What would make me happy," he said huskily, "is having you in my bed. Right now."

I sucked in my breath. My body trembled.

"No," I whispered.

His dark eyes met mine. "We both know how this will end."

He was right. *He was right.*

"Thank Maurine for me…." Setting down my silverware, I stumbled to my feet, tossing my napkin over my half-empty plate. "I'm done…."

And I ran.

Tears blurred my eyes as I fled the dining hall, into the shadowy hallway. I dodged antique chests and an old suit of armor, only to run straight into Maurine.

"My dear, whatever is the matter?" she said, looking astonished.

"I just need some—some fresh air," I choked out.

"Of course." Looking bewildered, with my baby still smiling and happy in her arms, she pointed to a door down the hall. "That leads to the gardens...."

I ran down the dark hallway, beneath the cool, thick stone walls of the *castillo*. Flinging open the door, I found myself beneath the bright, hot Spanish sun and the softly waving palm trees. I kept going, almost blindly—wanting only to be away from the castle. From the man who owned it.

Just as he now owned me.

But he would not own my heart, I vowed to myself, wiping my eyes. Not my heart and not my body...no matter how he might tempt me otherwise. I couldn't give in. I couldn't....

I ran down the stone path, past green hedges and huge oak trees with soft, full greenery, past a pond and a picturesque gazebo in an English-style garden, past something that looked like a hedge maze straight out of *Alice in Wonderland.* Choking out a sob, I abruptly stopped. I found myself in a rose garden, surrounded by a profusion of colorful blooms, gentle yellow, soft pink, innocent white and a blaze of red like heart's blood.

"Lena."

His voice was low behind me. Shocked, I whirled around.

"How did you...?"

Alejandro stood in front of me, dark and tall and powerful. Colorful roses and the primal green of the garden hemmed us in on every side, like a riotous jungle. "I know this garden. It's been my home since I was a child."

The sun left a frost of golden light against his dark hair, like a halo, tracing down the length of his body, his tanned, olive-toned skin, his sharp cheekbones, his hard-muscled body that moved with such sensual grace.

"I won't sleep with you," I breathed. "I won't!"

His cruel, sensual lips curved.

"We both know you will." I watched, mesmerized, as the words caused his tongue to flick against the edges of his lips, into the warm, dark honey of his mouth. I remembered how it had felt when he'd kissed me last night. My lips still felt bruised, from the sweet remnants of that fire. "You want me. As I want you."

"I won't let you take me because I am *conve-*

nient." I shook my head fiercely. "You can't have me now, Alejandro!"

He came closer, towering above me, our bodies so near they almost touched.

"Can't I?" he said huskily.

I stared up at him, shivering. Sunshine shimmered in the greenery around Alejandro, making the flowers gleam like colorful lights, the roses like tumbled scarlet against the deep forest green, the leaves and thorns and tangling vines.

Reaching out, he stroked a long tendril of my hair. "I wanted you from the moment I saw you in the hallways of that London mansion, watching me with such longing in your eyes." He lifted his gaze. "I wanted you then. I want you now. And I will have you."

His dark eyes were like deep pools, illuminated by streaks of amber in the sunlight. The kind of eyes that make you lose your breath, the kind a woman could drown in.

The kind of eyes that could make a woman forget a whole lifetime of grief and everything she should have learned from it.

He wanted me. The thought was like a flower. Like one of those beautiful, hardy, deeply poisonous oleander flowers I'd seen growing along the Spanish highway.

He wanted me.

"We are married now," he said.

"For Miguel's sake."

"*Sí.* We married for the sake of our son." He followed me, his powerful body intent, with his dark hair and his dark clothes, like a stalking panther. "But that is not why I want you in my bed."

"But I can't trust you—"

He straightened, his face dangerous. "Why do you think that?"

"You said you lied to me and will lie again. You said you're no good at keeping promises...."

Alejandro looked away. "That was about... something else." He looked back at me. "I will always keep my promises to you."

"But how can I believe that?" I whispered, my heart running like a scared deer.

"Because it's true." He moved closer, running his hand down my long, loose hair, down my back. I shivered beneath the soft, seductive touch. Lifting his hand, he stroked my cheek as he whispered, "Be with me. Be my wife."

My whole body trembled, leaning toward him.

"And if you still think you can't trust me..." His

fingers gently stroked my cheeks, lifting my chin as he said softly, "Trust this."

Lowering his head, he pressed his lips against mine. I felt his warmth, his power, the strength of his body. I closed my eyes, lost, dizzy with desire. When he finally pulled away, I stared up at him, trembling.

"Please," I choked out. I lifted my gaze to his. *Please don't make me love you.* "Please don't make me want you...."

He rubbed the pads of his thumbs along my swollen lower lip, and gave me a smile that was breathtaking in its masculine triumph. "Too late."

In the distance, I heard Maurine calling from the castle. I twisted my head, listening, and so did he.

Alejandro suddenly cupped my face in his hands. His eyes were dark. Merciless. "Tonight," he whispered. "You will be in my bed. Tonight..." He ran his fingertips down my shoulders, cupping my breasts. I gave a soft gasp, and he returned a sensual smile. "You will be my wife."

CHAPTER SEVEN

TONIGHT, YOU WILL be in my bed.

Tonight, you will be my wife.

The day raced by. I could not hold the hours back. The clock was ticking and when night fell, I knew he would take me, if not against my will, then at least against my heart.

The dinner table was busy and crowded and happy, because apparently Maurine, the daughter of American-Basque sheep ranchers, had gotten into the habit of eating with her entire household staff, many of whom lived in cottages on the edge of the Rohares estate, and their wives and children were always welcome, as well. Freshly made breads, fruit and cheese were spread across the table in a feast that also included meats, stews and seafood paella, and all kinds of desserts, *tortas* to *galletas*.

"You should see it on holidays," Maurine said to me with a smile, when she saw my eyes widen at the crowd that completely filled all the chairs at the table in the dining hall. "Then, everyone invites their extended families as well, and they come from all over Andalucía."

"Where on earth do they sit?"

Maurine's smile lifted to a grin. "We have to bring all the tables out of the attic and extra rooms, and bring in every antique chair we've got, and the old benches and chests."

"Nice," I murmured. I exhaled. "This place is amazing."

"Because of Alejandro." She looked a few places down the table, to where he was holding court with our baby son in his lap, introducing him to the families of household staff. The women were clustered around him, as if to offer obeisance to a visiting pasha. "He is my whole world. I owe him everything."

"I bet he'd say he owes everything to you. And looking at all this—" I looked at the food, at the decorations, at the care taken with all the details "—I'd have to agree."

"Oh, no." She shook her head vehemently. "If not for him, I never would have survived the aftermath of that car crash, when I lost my whole family…."

"I'm so sorry," I murmured. "I heard about that.

Losing your son and daughter-in-law, and even the housekeeper and her son.... I can't imagine how awful. But Alejandro lived."

"That's right. Yes." Shuddering, she closed her eyes. "He saved me. I can still see him in the hospital, his little, injured face covered with bandages, his eyes so bright. Bones in his face had been broken, and he'd never look the same, but he was worried about me, not himself. 'It'll be all right, Abuela,' he told me. 'I'm your family now.'" She blinked fast, her eyes sparkling with tears. "He gave me something to live for, when I wanted to die. And more." She shook her head. "He saved this castle. Even at twelve years old, he was determined to win back our family's lost fortune. He knew he could do it. And he wasn't afraid."

"No." Alejandro wasn't afraid of anything. And he always got what he wanted. I shivered, remembering the dark promise in his eyes in the garden. *Tonight, you will be in my bed. Tonight, you will be my wife....* I pushed the memory away. "How did he build a fortune out of nothing?"

"He went to Madrid at seventeen," Maurine said. "Worked eighteen-hour days, three different jobs. He took all the money he earned and poured it into risky investments that somehow paid off. He wasn't afraid to gamble. Or work. It just goes to show that nobility is in the heart," she said softly, almost as if she were talking to herself, "not the blood."

I snorted. "What are you talking about? He's the son of a duke. It doesn't get more noble than that."

Maurine abruptly focused her gaze on me. "Of course. That's what I meant. He's noble by birth."

Was she confused, or was she just confusing me? "Did people give you a hard time because of your background? I mean—" I shook my head awkwardly "—Alejandro said you grew up in the U.S., the daughter of sheep ranchers..."

"Shepherds, actually," she said, with a twinkle in her eye.

"Exactly. You were a regular girl—then you married a duke." I paused, trying to form the right words. "Did all the other aristocrats treat you badly? Did they call you a gold digger?"

"Me? No." She blinked, and her expression abruptly changed. "Oh, my dear. Is that what's been happening to you?"

I felt the color drain from my cheeks. "No, I..."

"Oh, you poor child." Her plump, wrinkled face was sympathetic, her blue eyes kind. She reached over and patted my hand. "Don't worry. You'll triumph over all the ugly, silly words that people can say. Alejandro loves you. And you love him. That's what matters."

Now my cheeks went hot. "Uh…"

"And I'm so happy you're part of our family." She gave my hand a little squeeze, then chuckled. "I was a little worried. You should have seen the women he dated before you. He didn't bring a single one home. For good reason. He knew I'd skewer them."

"I'm the first woman he ever brought home?" I said faintly.

She nodded. Her gaze became shadowed as she looked at Alejandro farther down the table. "I was starting to think he'd never let any woman into his heart. That he'd never let anyone know who he truly is." She gave me a sudden sharp look. "But you know. Don't you?"

I furrowed my brow. Was she talking about a biblical knowing? Otherwise I didn't really understand. "Um, yes?"

She stared at me, then releasing my hand, abruptly turned away. "How did you like the rose garden?"

I shivered in spite of myself. "It is…very beautiful," I managed. "Like paradise. But what were you saying about Alejandro...?"

Maurine's eyes shadowed. She bit her lip. "I can't believe you don't know. But if you don't, he has to be the one to..."

"Querida," I heard Alejandro say behind me. "It is time for bed."

Seriously? He was announcing this in front of his grandmother and the whole table? I turned with a scowl, then saw him holding up our sleepy-eyed son. Oh. He meant Miguel. With dinner served so late in Spain, it *was* past our baby's bed-time, and he was yawning in Alejandro's arms, causing dimples in his fat little cheeks. "Right." I held out my arms. "I need to give him a bath first...."

But Alejandro shook his head. He wasn't letting me escape so easily. "I'll help you. It's time I learned to do these things as well, don't you think?"

The gleam in his black eyes told me he knew I was scrambling to think of a way to avoid being alone with him tonight. Wondering if I could find a door with a lock. Surely there had to be one in this castle, with its choice of approximately five million rooms. I shook my head with an awkward laugh. "*You* don't want to learn how to give a baby his bath and put him to bed, Your Excellency!"

He snorted at that last bit. "A man needs to know how to take care of his own son." He lifted a dark eyebrow. "Don't you agree?"

"Yes," I grumbled.

"Such a good father," Maurine sighed.

I narrowed my eyes, then gave him a smile. "I'll show you how to change his diaper, too," I said sweetly.

He gave me a crooked grin. *"Excelente."*

A moment later, we were walking down the dark hallways, the noise of the happy dinner party receding behind us, beneath the thick inner walls of the castle.

"This way," he said, placing his fingertips innocently on the base of my spine to guide me. I trembled.

Tonight, you will be in my bed.

Tonight, you will be my wife.

"Our bedroom is in the new wing…."

"New wing?"

"This castle might have been home to this family for four hundred years, but antiques are—how shall I say this?—not my style."

Going up another flight of stairs, still holding

our baby protectively with his muscled arm, he pushed open the door at the end of that hall. I followed him inside, and saw an enormous, high-ceilinged room with floor-to-ceiling windows overlooking a balcony. Modern, masculine, stark. With only one real piece of furniture.

An enormous bed.

I stopped. "But where's the crib?"

"I've had the room next door turned into a nursery." To my relief, Alejandro didn't even glance at the big bed, but just kept walking straight into the connecting door that led to the nursery, and its en-suite bathroom.

The bathroom connected to the nursery was as severe and cold as the master bedroom had been, all white marble and gleaming chrome. But it did have an amazing view. Wide windows overlooked the dark vistas of his estate, lit only by moonlight and distant twinkling lights on the horizon.

He stopped, frowning at the marble bathtub. "On second thought, I don't think this is going to work," he said tersely, looking from the enormous tub to the baby in his arms. "He's too small. We need to get a special baby-size tub…."

It was endearing, really, to see how worried he was. "Tomorrow, if you like, we can go get one.

186 UNCOVERING HER NINE MONTH SECRET

For today, it's no problem." Smiling, I took Miguel in my arms. "Since he can't sit up on his own yet, we'll just hold him up. And be careful." Leaning over, I turned on the water. "Having an extra pair of hands will help."

His eyes met mine. "So you don't…mind that I'm helping you?"

"No," I said softly, "I'm glad."

His expression changed. He started to speak, then turned away, sticking his hand in the water. When the temperature was Goldilocks-acceptable—neither too hot nor too cold—he plugged the drain so the bathtub could fill.

Sitting the baby on the marble counter, I started to pull off his clothes and the clean diaper beneath. "Can you grab his baby shampoo? It's in my bag. Oh." I turned. "It's still in the car—"

With a grin, Alejandro held up the baby shampoo from a nearby drawer, along with a white, fluffy towel. "You mean this?"

"Oh," I said. My cheeks went hot. "It was nice of your staff to unpack everything for me, but…"

"But?"

"It's just strange to have someone going through my stuff."

"You'll get used to it. You'll never have to lift a

finger again, unless you want to. Especially with Abuela to oversee everything. She enjoys cooking, cleaning, shopping…" He paused, suddenly looking uncertain. "That is, if you wish that."

I lifted my eyebrows. "If I?"

Alejandro came closer to me.

"You are the duchess now," he said. "As far as the *castillo* is concerned, your rule is now law."

My cheeks went hot. I licked my lips, tried to laugh as I sat on the edge of the bathtub and checked the water with my elbow. "So you mean I could fire everyone, throw out your tenants, buy Maurine a condo in Barcelona, get rid of all the furniture and paint the walls pink?"

But he didn't laugh.

"If you like," he said in a low voice. "Though I'd prefer we keep the staff and tenants. If you decided otherwise, I would need to take care of them some other way."

"Give them all houses and jobs in Madrid?"

"Something like that."

This kind of thinking surprised me. Most of the high-powered CEO types I'd seen in New York and London seemed to constantly need to resole their expensive shoes, due to the wear caused by stepping on all the little people. I looked at Alejandro curiously. "You really feel responsible for them, don't you?"

"Of course. They—" Tightening his jaw, he looked away. "They're my people."

"Oh." I bit my lip. "Maybe you're not entirely the bastard I thought you were."

"But I am," he said in a low voice. He lifted his gaze to mine. "I can't change who I am."

Something about the expression of the chiseled lines of his handsome face made me feel all confused and jumbled inside. For a moment, the only sound between us was the water running into the bathtub, and the soft yawns of our baby.

"All right, fine. The staff can stay." I sighed. "It would probably be easier to just get rid of me, then."

His lips quirked upward. "Never. Sorry."

"Miguel is your responsibility. Not me," I pointed out. "You don't have to worry about me. I'm not…one of your people." I looked away. "I can support myself. Just so you know."

"I do know. I've seen your paintings."

I stiffened. Edward had often patronized my *little hobby.* "What is that supposed to mean?"

"Isn't it obvious? I think you're talented," he

said softly. He pointed toward the nursery. "Or didn't you notice?"

Frowning, I went to the door. And I sucked in my breath as I looked around the dark nursery, at the paintings lining the walls.

"You brought them," I whispered. "All the paintings from Mexico…all the pictures I did of Miguel since he was born."

"I wanted them here. With him." He looked at me. "With us."

A shiver went through me from deep inside.

"You are welcome to paint, or do any work you want," he said gravely, "but only if it nourishes your soul. And any money you make is exclusively your own."

"But that's not right. I don't expect you to support me, to support all of us—"

"That is my job," he said firmly, "to financially support you and Miguel and, God willing, other children."

Other children!

I swallowed, breathing hard. It was as if he were offering me everything I'd never dreamed I could ask for. After growing up an only child, an orphan, I'd always secretly yearned to have a large family. Now Alejandro didn't just want to be a father for Miguel. He wasn't offering just financial stability for us both. He wanted to give me more children, too.

And create those children inside me....

No! I had to get ahold of myself. No matter how Alejandro looked at me in the shadows, or how the husky sound of his voice made me tremble. No matter if he seemed to be offering me my dreams. Without love, without honesty, *it wouldn't work*.

I shook my head. "You don't need to do these things out of duty."

"Not duty." His hand cupped my cheek. "It is my honor. And more." His eyes met mine as he said huskily, "It is my pleasure."

My cheeks flamed with heat. Sparks of need crackled down my body from that single point of contact. My lips went dry, and tension coiled hot, deep inside.

Nervously, I pulled away, looking down at the enormous marble bathtub. "Water's ready."

I carried Miguel to the tub, and Alejandro was suddenly beside me, rolling up his long sleeves to reveal his powerful forearms, dusted with dark hair. "Allow me."

Together, we propped him up to sit in the few inches of water. Alejandro held him upright as I lathered up Miguel's soft, wispy dark hair. The baby was already yawning as we toweled him off, and got him into his blue footsie pajamas decorated with baby animals. He was half-asleep as I took him into the nursery, to cuddle him in a rocking chair and feed him before bed. Alejandro sat beside us in a cushioned window seat. His face was in silhouette as he watched us, with the wide view of the moon-swept valley and the distant lights of Seville.

I cuddled our baby close, until his eyes were heavy and his mouth fell off the nipple, though his plump mouth still pursed, drinking imaginary milk as he slept sweet baby dreams.

I finally rose to my feet.

"Can I put him to bed?" Alejandro said. "At least try…."

"Sure," I said softly. I handed him the burping cloth, then the fuzzy cuddle blanket. "But you'll need to burp him first."

"Um…I'm not so sure that's a…"

"You'll be fine." I lifted a sleepy Miguel against his shoulder, over the burping cloth, and showed him how to gently pat his small back. Hesitantly, Alejandro followed suit, until our baby came up with a huge burp, before he softly sighed, and his eyes became heavy again.

Alejandro flashed me a look of triumph. "Ha!"

Seeing him that way, this handsome, ruthless, broad-shouldered man holding his tiny sleeping son—our son—my heart twisted. I smiled, and hoped the dim light of the nursery wouldn't let him see how I was fighting tears.

Against everything I'd once believed, everything I'd once feared, Alejandro was an amazing father. I knew he would take care of Miguel and love him and always be there to catch him if he fell.

"Now what?" he whispered.

"Tuck him into the crib, on his back," I answered over the lump in my throat.

Alejandro moved slowly, careful not to wake Miguel, careful to hold his head. He looked as if he were sweating bullets, like a man under the pressure of disarming a nuclear weapon, as he gently set our baby down into his crib. Leaning over beside him, I placed Miguel's favorite baby blanket, the fuzzy one decorated with elephants, softly by his cheek.

For a long moment, we stood over the crib, watching our son slumber, listening to his quiet, even breathing. Then Alejandro lifted his head to look at me.

Our eyes locked. And what I saw in his face left me shivering beneath the open weight of his hunger. Wordlessly, he pulled me from the room, closing the door behind us.

We were alone. In his bedroom.

I stared at him, my heart pounding. "You have to know—what happened in the garden today was a mistake."

"*Sí,*" he agreed. "It was."

He was taking it a lot better than I'd thought he would. I exhaled. "So we won't…"

My voice trailed off as, for the first time, I realized someone had been in this bedroom while we'd been bathing Miguel. My eyes went wide.

A fire now crackled in the fireplace. Candles glowed from the marble mantle. And…no, surely it couldn't be…

Going toward the king-size bed at the center of the room, I picked up one of the scarlet, fragrant petals that had been scattered over the white bedspread.

"Rose petals?" I said dumbly. Turning, I held it up. "I don't understand…."

He gave a low, sensual smile. "Don't you?"

I exhaled. "You arranged this."

"Yes."

"But you just agreed that our kiss was a mistake—"

"It shouldn't have happened in the garden. Or the kiss in the coatroom in Madrid, either. I wanted you. I lost control. That was the mistake." Coming close to me, he shook his head. "But this won't be."

"Don't look at me like that," I whispered.

"Like what?"

"Like..." I licked my lips. "Like it's all you can do to keep yourself from ripping off my clothes and sliding me beneath you..."

"Because, *querida,*" he said, cupping my face, "it is. I've dreamed of you for so long...."

"You dreamed of me?" I breathed, remembering all the nights I'd yearned for him, in hot dreams that had made me ache, only to wake up bereft and cold in the morning.

"Yes. But tonight, *querida,* tonight," he whispered, lowering his head toward mine, "my dreams come true. Not for duty. Not for convenience. But for pleasure. For need." He slowly traced his hand down the side of my body. "There's been no one for me since you, Lena. Did you know that? No other woman I've wanted in my bed. Just you. And now you are mine at last—as I am yours…."

As the fire crackled in the fireplace, I saw the shadows of red and orange move across the hard edges and planes of his handsome, saturnine face.

"It can't be true."

He pulled me into his arms.

"Tonight," he said softly, "will be the first night of forever."

Trembling, I looked up into his dark eyes. I tried to think of something, anything, to send him away from me. I tried to make my body move away, to run. But it was no longer obeying me. My body knew what it wanted. What it had always wanted.

I felt his hands tighten on my back, over the fabric of my blouse, as he pulled me close.

And he lowered his head to mine. I felt the warmth of his breath against my skin. A hard, reckless shiver went up and down my body. Of need. Of desire so great it made me shake.

Because what I wanted now, though beautiful as flowers, could poison my soul, and kill my heart. Just like the oleander…

"Please," I breathed as I felt the roughness of his jawline brush against my cheek. It was all I could do, to keep from leaning into him, kissing him, pulling him hard and tight against me. I wanted him so badly, I could almost have wept from it.

He traced his fingertip very gently from my earlobe, along my cheek, to my full, aching lower lip. "Please?"

"Please…" I tried to remember what I wanted. *Please kiss me. Please don't.*

But he didn't give me time to gather my senses. Lowering his mouth to my ear, he whispered, "You are mine. Forever and always. My pleasure. My duchess. My wife. My lover…"

"No," I whispered. "I can't be…."

"I forgot." He drew back, his eyebrows an amused slash over his heavy-lidded eyes. "You said you do not want me."

"I don't," I said, praying he would believe such a lie.

"I see." He ran his hand down the bare skin to my throat. "So you feel nothing when I do this…."

Trembling, I shook my head.

"And this…" His large hand cupped my breast over my blouse, the tip of his thumb rubbing over my nipple, which pebbled, aching and taut beneath the fabric.

I couldn't speak. I looked up at him, my lips parted, my heart pounding.

"Give in. To me."

"But I don't love you," I choked out, but what that really meant was *Don't make me love you.*

"I do not ask for your heart. But your body—*sí*. Tonight…your body will be mine."

And he lowered his mouth to mine.

His lips were gentle, even tender. One touch, and I was proved a liar. Of course I wanted him. Of course I did.

I sighed, as his kiss deepened, became demanding, hungry. My arms wrapped around his shoulders, pulling him close.

He slowly lowered me back against the enormous bed covered with rose petals. I gloried in the heavy weight of his body over mine, pressing me deep into the soft mattress.

He pulled off my blouse, kissing down my body as each opened button revealed more of my skin. He lifted me against him, to pull off my shirt. I felt the warmth of his fingertips trailing down my naked arms, down my back. With expert precision, he unlatched my bra with a single flick of his fingers, and my breasts hung free, full and heavy and aching for his touch.

I heard the hoarseness of his breath as he pushed me back against the bed. Cupping my breasts with his hands, he nuzzled between them, lowering his head to one taut nipple, then the other, pulling it gently into his mouth as I gasped with pleasure.

"Wait," I choked out. "I want to feel you—"

Reaching for his shirt, I yanked it hard from his body. I was definitely not as careful as he'd been about the buttons. At least one ripped off entirely and scattered noisily against the floor in my desperation to feel the warmth of his skin. I exhaled when I could at last run my hands over his naked chest, feeling his hard sculpted muscles beneath the light dusting of dark hair. A low groan came from his lips, and he fell against me on the bed, ravishing my lips with his own.

Ohhhh… Deeper, deeper. The pleasure of his tongue against mine, his lips hard and so sweet, made me burn all over, made me lose my mind….

He kissed slowly down my bare skin, working his way to my belly button, which he flicked with his tongue. Unbuttoning my jeans, he rolled them with my panties down my hips, peeling the fabric inch by inch down my legs, kissing and licking and nibbling as he went, until I was naked and gasping for breath.

He kissed the hollow of my foot, then gently pushed my legs wide. From the base of the bed, he looked up at me, spread-eagled across the bed, naked for his pleasure. I quivered with need. If he tried to leave me now—my lips parted. In that moment, I would have done anything—begged, even—to get him to stay.

But no begging was necessary. With a low growl, he removed his own trousers and then fell hard and naked upon me. I felt the length of him, like steel, pressing between my legs. Looking up at his face in the flickering shadows of the firelight, I realized that he wasn't in nearly as much control of himself as I'd imagined. In fact, he was barely keeping himself in check.

"You don't have to hold back," I choked out, pulling him down against me, my hips lifting of their own volition against his. "Please…"

And this time, there was no question what I wanted. But he would not let me control him or set the pace. Shrugging off my grasp, he slid down my body, then parted my legs with his shoulders at my knees. I felt the heat of his breath against my inner thighs. I gasped, reaching my hands out to grip the white comforter beneath me.

Pressing his large hands against my thighs, he spread me wide. He lowered his head and took a long, languorous taste.

My hips bucked beneath his tongue. The pleasure was almost too much to bear. I tried to move away. But he held me fast. He stroked me, licked me, leaving me wet and in the agony of almost unbearable pleasure. His sensual tongue flicked against my taut core, and I held my breath, tilting my head back, my eyes rolling back in my head as I lifted higher, and tighter.

The moment before I would have exploded, he pulled back. I whimpered. I heard his low laugh as he changed position, returning his mouth to where it had been, but pressing his hands beneath my backside to hold me hard against him. Spreading his mouth wide, he worked me with his tongue, going wide, then deep, then wide again. I felt his tongue thrust inside me, and cried out. My back arched against the mattress as he forced me to accept the pleasure, and as he proved to me, against my will, how much more of it my body could endure.

With a single ragged breath, I lifted higher, and higher, but again, just as I was about to explode, he lifted his mouth. He smiled down at me.

By this point I was starting to turn to a mindless mess, somewhere between blubbering and wanting to resort to physical violence, because I knew he was teasing me, forcing me to soar, to coast, then soar higher still.

Abruptly, he lifted my legs to wrap around his tight, trim hips. Rose petals flew up from the bed as he moved me, the flowers leaving a sensual, heady fragrance as they fell back to earth, sliding first against his body, then mine. I felt him pressing hard and stiff and huge between my legs. I exhaled, pressing my fingers into his back, nearly weeping with need.

Again, he started to pull away, but this time, I wouldn't let him go. My fingernails dug into the skin of his back, and I gave a low growl. *"Bien, querida,"* he panted. *"Bien."*

He positioned his hips, and in one rough movement, he shoved himself inside me, hard and thick and enormous, ramming himself to the hilt. That very first thrust made me explode from the inside out. I saw stars as waves of bliss shook through me. I heard a rising animal cry and realized to my shame that it came from my mouth. I fell back against the soft mattress, as if from a far distance, landing a limp heap on his bed.

He froze, still deep inside me in that first thrust.

"You can go on…" I panted, trying to catch my breath. "I already…"

"More," he said, eyeing my face hungrily. "Do it again."

Again? Was he crazy? I shook my head. "I can't…"

"Again," he said grimly.

He slowly pushed inside me, this time letting me feel every inch. He made me stretch for him, as I felt him deep inside. It felt good. But he was holding himself back for no reason. I knew there was no way I could…

Drawing back, he slowly filled me again, and then again. Gripping my shoulders tight with his hands, he rode me. To my amazement, a new tension began to build deep inside me. Different this time. Even deeper. With a gasp, I wrapped my hands around him, feeling the clench and un-clench of the muscled cheeks of his backside, feeling the sweat on his skin as he fiercely held himself in check.

His thrusts became rougher as he rode me harder, faster, our sweaty naked bodies sliding against each other. He held my shoulders tight enough to bruise, as he pounded me hard, hard, hard. Deep, deep, deep. My back started to arch again. Seeing that, he sucked in his breath and lowered his lips to mine, kissing me. I felt the flick of his tongue against mine as he rammed into me so deep, and that was it—the brutality and force and lust shook me into an explosion so great I screamed into his mouth.

His self-control evaporated. With a low guttural growl, he shoved into me one last time, and with a gasp and groan, he spent himself inside me.

He collapsed, his body heavy over mine on the bed.

It took long moments for me to return back to earth. When I did, my eyes flew open.

"We forgot to use a condom," I blurted out. I expected him to look horrified. He did not.

"I forgot nothing." He gave me a heavy-lidded smile. "I want to get you pregnant, Lena."

Shock went through me as I stared at him with wide eyes. "But we…"

"I will fill you with my child, *mi esposa*. Try to fight me if you must," he whispered, then his smile lifted to a grin. "It is always a pleasure to battle with you."

CHAPTER EIGHT

SUNSHINE WAS SPILLING from the windows, across our naked, intertwined bodies spread across the bed, the white cotton sheets twisted and tangled at our feet. My first thought when I woke was to think it all had been a dream. Then I saw Alejandro, still sleeping in my arms, a soft smile on his chiseled face.

I caught my breath. My heart beat faster, in a rhythm like music, because joy—pleasure—everything I'd ever wanted had all come true at once.

Slowly, Alejandro opened his eyes, and his smile widened. His expression was open, and young, and he, too, seemed to be shining with happiness. *"Buenos días,"* he whispered, leaning forward to kiss me tenderly on the forehead, *"mi corazon."*

"Good morning." I blushed, looking away, feeling oddly shy.

Reaching out, he lifted my chin and kissed me, until all thoughts of shyness disappeared beneath the mutual hunger building anew between us.

How was it possible? We'd made love three times last night—three times!—and yet he was still brand new. I gloried in his touch, in the feel of his naked, hard-muscled body against mine, his arms holding me as if I were truly the precious names he'd called me. *My pleasure, my duchess, my wife. My lover.*

And now something more. Something new he'd called me for the first time.

My heart...

We made love once more, hot, hard and fast— and good thing about that last bit, because thirty seconds after we'd both collapsed in a sweaty, gasping heap on top of each other, I heard an indignant cry from the nursery.

We looked at each other and laughed.

"I'll get him," I said, starting to rise from the bed.

"No." He put his hand on my shoulder, pressing me back against the soft sheets, and rose from the bed, pulling on a white terry-cloth robe over his hard-muscled body. "You got up last time. Relax. Go take a shower. Take your time."

I came out, hot and clean and pink-cheeked and happy. I got dressed in a soft pink shirt and skirt, and fed the baby as my husband had a shower in his turn.

This was just as I'd always dreamed. No. It was better. Just the three of us...

For now.

My hand slowly fell on my belly. *I want to fill you with my child.* Was I afraid? Yes. But did I also want, desperately want, another baby? Also yes.

So much had changed since the last time I was pregnant. Instead of being a fearful fugitive, I was married now. Settled. With a home.

Would it be so wrong to just let myself be happy? Alejandro was a good father. He was proving to be a good husband. He wanted to take care of me forever. He wanted us to be a family. And the way he made love to me... I shuddered at the memory of ecstasy.

Would it be so forbidden, so foolish, to trust my husband with my heart?

If only I knew the lie he was telling me, or had told, or would tell. He said he'd been faithful to me for a year, that he'd never be disloyal.

Of course, that could be the lie....

My lips pressed together, and I grimly pushed the thought away. I told myself that, since he'd shared so much of his body, surely he'd soon find it irresistible to share the secrets of his heart. And then I forced myself not to think about it.

Denial is a beautiful thing. A woman in love can be very good at focusing on the rose and ignoring the thorn—at least until it draws blood. Over breakfast, I kept smiling at Alejandro over my plate of eggs and *jamón,* my coffee diluted with tons of cream and sugar. And instead of treating me like a lovesick fool, as I no doubt looked like, Alejandro, the dark, dangerous, ruthless duke, did the unthinkable.

He kept smiling back.

"I'd like to take you around the estate today," he said, sipping his black coffee and reading the morning newspaper, "to meet my tenants."

"What?" I nearly dropped the baby rattle I'd been holding out for Miguel, who was sitting in my lap. Chortling, the baby grabbed it in his fat little fist and triumphantly began to shake. "I thought I'd meet them at the wedding reception."

"Abuela told me it will take her two months to plan the reception. We cannot wait that long." His eyes met mine. He seemed to sense my fear, because he gave me an encouraging smile. "You are my wife. It is right that I introduce you to the tenants on the estate. That is the merest good manners."

"But…"

"Besides. Knowing Abuela, the reception will be a lavish affair, to impress acquaintances and friends. I want the first introduction to be private. Personal." He paused. "Many of them have been farming this land for generations. They might have heard rumors. They might think that having a baby first, and getting married second, is a little…"

"Modern?" I supplied.

"Yes. Modern. I don't want them to wonder if this is a real marriage, or if we'll stand the test of time."

"Will we?" I whispered.

"We will," he said seriously, looking straight into my eyes. "And I want them to have no doubt you are here to stay." Leaning forward, he took my hand in his own. "I want them to think well of you, as I do." He looked at me. "Will you meet them?"

Having Alejandro look at me with his deep dark eyes, and hold my hand, and ask me something, in his husky voice, there was no possibility of resistance. No matter how the thought of trying to impress a bunch of strangers and convince them I would make an excellent *duquesa* filled me with dread. What if they thought I wasn't good enough? What if they had such deep doubts, Alejandro changed his mind about me and decided to find some other wife more worthy? "All right," I said hesitantly. "If you think it truly necessary."

"I do." Alejandro's eyes softened as he looked at our baby. "I'd like Miguel to come, as well. Because he is their future. And they are his."

I bit my lip, trying my best not to look nervous. "Right. Four hundred years on this land, right? So it's in Miguel's blood."

"Something like that." Alejandro put down his napkin and rose to his feet. "We'll see the Widow Ramirez first. She was my governess, once."

The thought warmed my heart. "She taught you as a child?"

"Both me and the…housekeeper's son."

"You mean Miguel," I said softly. "Your friend."

"Yes. We played together as children, studied together, fought. It didn't matter that one of us was a future duke and the other just the housekeeper's son. We studied the same subjects, lived in the same house. We both loved Abuela. We were friends. Until Miguel died that day."

"And you survived," I said gently, touching his shoulder.

"Yes. I survived." He turned away. "I'll get the keys."

I finished my breakfast and my orange juice. When Alejandro returned, he said, "Señora Ramirez is no longer as sharp as she used to be, but she still has a lot of influence with the other tenants."

"No pressure," I muttered, my heart suddenly cold with fear. I looked down at my pink shirt and floppy cotton skirt. "Maybe I should change."

He barely glanced at me. "You're fine."

"I want them to like me...."

Alejandro laughed. "Fancy clothes won't make them like you. In fact, if you showed up in a designer dress and five-inch stiletto heels, they'd like you *less*. The farmers respect honesty, hard work and kindness when it's called for. Bluntness when it's not." His dark eyes gleamed. "You should get along just fine."

"Oh, all right," I sighed, sure he was wrong.

A half hour later, the three of us were in his estate vehicle, a black, open-air Jeep, headed over a dirt road that crossed the wide fields and hills belonging to the Castillo de Rohares.

The Widow Ramirez's house was a snug little cottage on the edge of the estate, where she grew organic peaches and persimmons, aubergines and artichokes, and raised goats that produced milk and cheese. Frail and wizened, barely as tall as my shoulder, when she answered her door she looked at me with critical, beady eyes. But by the end of the visit, she was smiling and pushing more of her homemade butter cookies toward me.

"Eat, eat," she pleaded. "You must keep up your strength if you are to give your husband more children."

I felt Alejandro looking at me, and blushed.

"*Gracias,* Pilar," he said, putting his hands on my shoulders. "We wish for more children very much."

"Of course you do," she said, pouring him tea. "I know it was always your desire to have a larger family, growing up so lonely, up in that huge castle, with your older sister off working in Granada. And your mother," she sniffed, "working night and day, when she wasn't distracted by the duke...."

"Sister? What sister? Alejandro is an only child," I added, frowning up at him. "Aren't you?"

He cleared his throat, glancing at his old governess. "You're confused, Pilar," he said gently. "You're thinking of Miguel. Not me."

Her rheumy eyes focused on him. Then she nearly jumped in her chair. "Yes. Yes, of course. That was Miguel. You are El Duque." She abruptly held out a plate to me. *"¿Más galletas?"*

"Yes, please."

She beamed at me. "It makes me so happy you like my cookies. Alejandro—" she looked at him severely "—barely ate one."

He laughed. "I had three."

"Hardly any," she sniffed. She smiled at me. "You should take the example of your wife, and eat four or more."

"Gracias," I said happily, and took another one, buttery and flaky and sweet. "I will need this recipe."

"I'll be delighted to send it to you!"

Shortly afterward, as we rose to leave, Alejandro hugged the widow's small frame gently and looked at her with real love. "Take care of yourself, Pilar. We'll see you soon."

"You, too, M—Alejandro." Shaking her head with a wry smile, she reached up and patted his cheek, then looked down and kissed the top of our baby's head. Looking among the three of us, she said, "I'm so happy for you, my dear. How it's all turned out. You deserve a happy life."

Leaving her cottage, we got back into his open Jeep, tucking Miguel into the baby seat in the backseat. As we drove across the bumpy road, I exhaled in pure relief. Closing my eyes, I turned my face up to the warm morning sun, feeling happy that I'd somehow—I had no idea how— passed the first test. Instead of her tossing me out, she'd fed me cookies. And I'd pretty much eaten all of them. What can I say? They were delicious. I really did need that recipe.

Smiling, I turned to look at my husband. "She was nice."

"I'm glad you think so." He was looking at me with a strange expression, as if he wanted to say something. I frowned, and I parted my lips to ask what he was thinking. Before I could, he looked away.

"We'll visit the Delgado family next."

For the rest of the day, as my confidence built, I spoke with all of the tenants on his estate. They seemed relieved and happy that I spoke Spanish, though they took pleasure in teasing me merci- lessly about my accent. They adored the baby, and all of them praised my new husband to me, even when he was out of earshot. One after another, they told me stories of his noble character, his good heart.

"The land was neglected, and El Duque brought it back from the brink...."

"My roof was falling apart, but El Duque helped me fix it...."

"When the crop died, I thought I would have to leave. But El Duque gave me a loan, enough for seed and animals. He saved us, and he himself was only eighteen...."

"He gave my son a job in Madrid, when there were no jobs to be had. José would have left for Argentina." The old woman wiped her eyes. "El Duque kept my son here in Spain, and I'm so grateful. I'll never forget...."

By the time we visited the last house in early evening, I was no longer even nervous. I was relaxed, holding our baby, laughing and chatting with the farmers, complimenting them on their well-cared-for fields and animals, complimenting their wives on their delicious *tartas*. And seeing how they admired Alejandro, how they treated him with such respect. His people did love him.

And by extension, I realized, they were willing to love me, for his sake. And for the sake of our child.

On the drive back home over the dusty road, back to the castle at the top of the hill, we didn't speak in the open-air Jeep. Miguel was sleeping in the back. Finally, I smiled at Alejandro. "That went well, don't you think?"

"Yes," he said shortly.

What could he possibly be mad about now? Biting my lip, I looked at the passing scenery. I was already starting to love Spain, especially Andalucía. The air was warm, dusty from our tires on the dirt road. The sun was starting to fade to the west, leaving a soft golden glow across the fields. I felt the warm breeze against my skin, the air scented by honeysuckle and bougainvillea and the jacaranda trees in bloom.

But Alejandro didn't say a word. He pulled the truck in front of the garage. Getting out, he opened my door. When I stepped out of the Jeep, he pulled me into his arms. I looked up at him, biting my lip. "Alejandro, didn't I do—all right?"

"All right?" he said huskily. I saw the warmth in his deep brown eyes. They held the same glow as the soft Andalucían morning. "I am proud of you beyond words, *mi corazon*. You made them love you. As..."

He cut himself off, but as I looked up at his face, my heart started to pound. "They loved me for your sake."

"No." He shook his head. "They loved you only for yourself. Your warmth, your smile, your..." Reaching down, he stroked my cheek. Something seemed to stretch tight between us, making me hold my breath. His hand trailed down my hair, down my back. "Come upstairs with me," he whispered. "Right now..."

"But dinner..."

He lowered his head to mine in a deep, passionate kiss, taut and tender, slow and sweet. I clutched his shoulders, lost in his embrace.

Miguel gave a plaintive whine from the back of the Jeep, and Alejandro released me with a rueful laugh. "But Abuela will be expecting us for dinner."

"Yes." I shook my head with a snort. We'd been fed at literally every house we visited. "I won't be able to eat a bite. I'm not the least bit hungry."

"Funny. I'm starving." He gave me a dark look that made my body burn, and I knew he wasn't talking about food. He sighed grumpily.

"But you're right. Dinner has been arranged. We wouldn't want to disappoint Abuela...."

"No. We wouldn't." I took our baby out of the truck, and we went upstairs to give Miguel his bath. Alejandro left to dress for dinner tonight, as Maurine had requested. I fed our baby, cuddling him in the rocking chair as he drifted off to sleep, plump and adorable in his footsie pajamas, holding his soft blanket against his cheek. I finally tucked him into his crib, then went to the master suite next door.

I felt dusty from the road, and was tempted to take a shower, but feared that would make me late, which would be rude. Especially since Maurine had insisted tonight's dinner was special somehow. So I just brushed out my hair and put on a long slinky dress and high heels. She'd asked us to dress up for dinner tonight, though what made tonight different from the other nights, I had no idea. I put on some red lipstick and looked at myself in the mirror. I looked so different, I thought. I barely recognized myself. I tossed my hair, seeing the bold new gleam in my eye—and liking it.

Smiling, I went downstairs. But as I walked down the sweeping stairs, voices echoed from the shadows of the stairwell below.

"You should tell her the truth." Maurine's voice was uncharacteristically sharp.

"No," Alejandro answered coldly.

"She's your wife—"

"She cannot know. Not yet. Perhaps not ever. I don't know if I can trust her."

"But this is your life we're talking about!"

"Not just my life. Also yours. And Miguel's. She could destroy us all if she—"

Then they looked up and saw me. I shaped my mouth into a bright smile, as if I hadn't heard anything, as if my heart wasn't pounding.

"You look spectacular, *mi esposa*," Alejandro murmured, and held out his arm. He was dressed in a dark tailored shirt and trousers. "May I escort you to dinner?"

I nodded. But as we walked down the hallway toward the banqueting hall, the happiness that had been building inside me all day had suddenly gone *pfffft* like a balloon.

What was he hiding?

It was growing harder to push the question from my mind. Even denial will carry you only so far. My recent happiness suddenly felt like a house of cards waiting to fall.

I'd felt such incandescent joy, being in his arms

last night. Being by his side today, meeting his neighbors and the people who mattered to him. Being introduced, with pride, as his wife.

Every moment I spent with him, I was falling deeper and deeper into an emotion I'd sworn I'd never feel for him again. Especially since I knew he was lying to my face. I was walking straight into heartbreak, only this time, I'd have no one to blame but myself.

Abruptly, I stopped in the middle of the hallway.

He frowned down at me. "What, *querida?*"

I looked at him, my heart aching. "I need to know what you're hiding from me."

Setting his jaw, he shook his head.

"I wish I'd never told you," he said harshly. Dropping my hand, he looked at me with cold eyes. "Should we spend dinner apart?"

He was ruthlessly ending the conversation. Swallowing back tears, I shook my head. He held out his arm again.

We walked, the only sound our footsteps against the flagstones. "I wonder why Maurine insisted that we dress up for dinner tonight," I said over the awkward silence. "I just saw her wearing an old cardigan and jeans...."

We entered the banqueting hall, and my voice cut off.

It was completely empty of other people. The only light came from the blazing fire in the enormous stone fireplace. Tall tapered candles lit the table. Beneath the high, timbered ceilings, the shadows and fire made the room breathlessly romantic.

I blinked, bewildered. "This is why Maurine wanted us to dress for dinner...?" Then Alejandro gave me a sensual smile, and it all clicked into place. "You arranged this," I breathed.

He shrugged. "I spoke with her before we left this morning, and she agreed newlyweds need time alone."

"But what about dinner for everyone else?"

"They already ate." He came closer, his dark eyes intent. "And I'm glad," he said huskily. "I want you to myself."

I stared at him, still conflicted about the way he'd coldly cut off my earlier question. Going to the table, he poured us each a glass of red wine that sparkled like a ruby in the firelight.

"Manzanilla wine. From my vineyard."

As we sat next to each other at the end of the long table, near the fire, I felt my anger starting to be melted by his nearness. The dinner was probably delicious, but I ate mechanically, barely tasting it. Alejandro moved his chair closer. He did not try to touch me. He started asking me questions, asking what I thought of Spain, how I liked the estate, how I liked the baby's nursery. He asked me how I'd first started painting.

"My father taught me," I said softly. "He always wanted to be an artist. But once he got married and had a family, he had to try to earn a living...." I gave a rueful laugh. "He was never good at earning money. But we loved him, just as he was."

Alejandro leaned forward, his elbow on the table, his chin resting on his hand, listening to every word. He focused his attention on me, as if nothing and no one else existed.

I knew how this worked. I'd seen it before. And yet I still could not resist. With every breath I felt him seducing me, drawing me in closer. Against my will, my heart started to warm.

The enormous banqueting hall, usually chilly inside the castle even on a hot summer day, was growing increasingly hot. I found myself leaning forward, asking him questions in my turn, and all the while wishing he would kiss me, and hating myself for wanting it. Finally, I could bear it no longer.

"Why can't you tell me your secret?"

"Put it from your mind," he said harshly. "Or go."

"Fine," I said tearfully. I stood, turning away.

He grabbed me by the wrist.

Slowly, Alejandro rose from the chair, his body grazing mine as he fully stood, towering over me. My head tilted back to look at his face. He was bigger than me, stronger by far. But it wasn't his strength that overwhelmed me, but the stark vulnerability I suddenly saw in his hard, handsome face.

"This is all you need to know," he whispered.

He pushed me against the edge of the stone fireplace, holding my wrists above me, kissing my lips, my throat. Closing my eyes, I tilted back my head as waves of desire crashed over me.

"I want you, Lena," he whispered, his voice husky, his lips brushing my earlobe. *"Te deseo."*

I shivered. Then remembered why I was mad at him and tried to pull away. "I—I am dusty and sweaty from the road." I gave a casual laugh that no one would believe, least of all me. "I rushed downstairs because I didn't want to be late."

He continued to kiss my face, and I closed my eyes, breathing, "But I should…really…go take a bath…."

"Bien," he purred. "I'll join you."

My eyes flew open. "A shower, I mean, not a bath," I stammered. "There's not much room in the shower for two…."

He ran his hands down my back, holding me against him. "Just enough."

He kissed me, and beneath the sensuality of his embrace, I sighed, and my lips parted. My body melted into his, my soft curves pressing into his hard angles as if his body had been made for mine.

Lifting me into his arms as if I weighed nothing at all, he carried me upstairs to our private, luxurious bathroom, where he gently set me on my feet. His dark eyes never left mine as he slowly pulled off my dress, then my bra, then my panties.

When I was completely naked in front of him, he wrenched me hard against him and kissed me deeply, hungrily. I desperately began to unbutton his shirt, then his trousers, until he, too, was naked.

Pulling away, he turned on the water in the shower. I glanced back longingly at the bed, but it was in the next room and seemed a million miles away. He kissed me again, and I gasped against his lips, his naked body hard against mine. Steam lifted from the hot water of the shower, making the luxurious bathroom of white marble and silver a magical, otherworldly place of ice and snow.

Except for the heat. Every inch of me felt warm, bursting with fire.

Alejandro pulled me into the shower. He pushed me away from him firmly, and I whimpered.

"Patience," he said, and I could almost hear his smile. He was still in control. Unlike me...

With agonizing slowness, he washed me in the shower, tangling shampoo in my hair, rubbing soap over my body, scrubbing every inch of me. I felt him stroke my full, naked breasts, my waist, my hips, the soft hair between my legs. I closed my eyes, swaying on my feet. I felt hot and unsteady as he caressed my hair, down my earlobes, my neck. I left handprints in the glass wall of the shower, against the white steam.

Turning me around to face him, he ran his hands down my breasts, over my belly, over my hips and thighs. Hot shooting streams of water poured over us both.

And he knelt before me. Gently parting my thighs, he pressed his face between my legs.

I gasped. His lips were tender and sensual and warm. His tongue slid against me, inside me, the merest breath of a stroke, hot and wet beneath the warm water.

I closed my eyes, pressing my hands against the glass wall behind me.

His hands slid around me, holding me firmly against his mouth. He teased me with the tip of his tongue, soft and light against the most sensitive part of me, then spread me wide and lapped me, until I tossed back my head, slapping my long wet hair against the glass as I shook all over. The hot, steamy water poured over us both as I felt his hands—his tongue—slide over my wet, pink skin.

For an intoxicating eternity, he teased me, bringing me almost to an explosion of pleasure beneath the steamy pulse of the shower, then backing away the very second before I would have exploded into bliss. It might have been seconds or hours, that he seduced me with this sweet torment.…

When my need was too much to bear, and I was shaking so hard I could barely breathe with desire, Alejandro turned me around, pressing me against the glass, my bottom resting against his hard, thick length.

"You're mine," he growled in my ear. "Say it."

"I'm yours," I breathed, pressing my arms against the glass.

"Again."

"I'm yours!"

"Forever."

"Forever," I whispered.

He thrust inside me roughly, deep and hard, and I gasped.

I forgot everything in the overwhelming pleasure of having him inside me. *Pleasure* was not a big enough word for it. I melted, lost myself, found myself, until he exploded inside me, and I soared.

Afterward, both of us were panting and spent, and he abruptly turned off the water. He opened the shower door and toweled me off. Without a word, he lifted me in his arms and carried me to our enormous bed. Looking back, I saw the trail of water he'd left across his stark floor.

Clinging to my husband's naked chest as he carried me, I felt as if I were in another time or place. I wondered dreamily about other lovers who'd done this, hundreds of years ago, in this very castle, when the sultan ruled.

Setting me down naked on our bed, he looked down at me. I smiled up at him, blinking tears of emotion, of anger and joy all mixed up together.

Climbing beside me, he held me, kissing my temple tenderly. Our bodies intertwined, his wet skin sliding against mine. My hand stroked the hardness of his chest, laced with dark hair. He held me tight. My eyes were heavy, and started to close.

I'd told him the truth in the shower.

I was his.

Now and forever.

Because I love him....

The realization hit like a bolt of lightning, causing my eyes to fly open.

I was in love with him, and there was something he was keeping from me. A reason he was lying. A secret he thought would hurt me.

I was in love with my husband.

But if I knew the secret he hid from me, would that love be destroyed?

CHAPTER NINE

THE NEXT FEW weeks fled by in a blur. We spent our days doing the work of the estate, talking to tenants and managing the house. I started painting in the garden in the morning, and played with our baby on the floor of Alejandro's home office as he worked on the computer and spoke on the phone to employees around the world.

"I begrudge them every hour," he told me, stroking my cheek. "I would rather spend it with you."

My heart sang as the birds did, flying free through the lush green trees, across the wide blue Spanish sky. But eventually, Alejandro had to go on a business trip. "Madrid?" I pouted.

He laughed. "Granada."

"Isn't that where the Alhambra is?" I said eagerly, picturing the famous Moorish castle. "I'll come with you!"

He shook his head. "It will be a one-day trip, there and back. Very boring. Stay here with Miguel. Paint. Enjoy your day." He kissed my temple and said huskily, "I'll be back before bed-time."

Then he kissed me *adios* until my toes curled.

But after he'd gone, all the fears and shadows came back crashing around me, without Alejandro's warmth and strength to hide behind.

Was he really going to do business in Granada, as he'd said? Or was he there for some other reason?

Was this his lie?

Don't think about it, I ordered my trembling heart, but it was impossible, now that I loved him.

I feared knowing the truth.

I feared never knowing it.

"Dear?" I heard Maurine's tremulous voice. "I wonder if I could ask you a favor?"

"Of course," I said, desperate for distraction.

She smiled at me. "You are such a talented artist. I love the paintings you've done of my roses. You are the only one who's ever done them justice." As I blushed, she continued, "Alejandro's birthday is next month. Would you do a portrait of me and Miguel, in the rose garden...?"

"I'd love to!" I exclaimed, my mind immediately filled with painting materials, size and composition. I went into Seville for supplies, and by late afternoon, after Miguel's nap, the three of us were outside. I propped up an easel in front of where they sat on a bench, surrounded by greenery and red, yellow and pink roses.

The warm Spanish sun filtered golden light over the garden as I painted the portrait of the dowager Duchess of Alzacar and her great-grandbaby, the future duke.

Maurine's lovely white hair was like a soft cloud around her twinkling eyes and smiling face. I drew her outline in loose strokes. That was easy, compared with the challenge of the wiggling, giggling baby in her lap. But I'd painted and drawn my son so many times over the past six months, I knew his chubby face by heart. I could have done it blindfolded.

I smiled to myself, picturing how happy Alejandro would be at the gift, reaching up to adjust the floppy pink hat I was wearing to keep the sunlight out of my eyes. Maurine chattered nonstop, while entertaining the baby in her lap. She told me how she'd first fallen in love with her husband, who'd had a title, "though it seemed useless enough, with no hope of returning to Spain, with the political situation," and absolutely no money or marketable skills. "It's so much easier to know how to work when you've been raised to it. My husband had spent his adult life sleeping in the spare rooms of rich friends from his Eton days."

"Sounds like my father. He wanted to work, but didn't know how."

"It's the upbringing, I think. Even when we finally returned to Spain, with the Navaro fortune lost, Rodrigo had no idea how to pay for the upkeep of this castle. It's not like the old days, when a duke could simply demand peasants give him tribute." She gave a soft laugh. "He was desperate to keep the title and the land, for the sake of his family's history. I loved him, so I did my best to help." She looked away, blinking fast. "I sold oranges from the orchard and gave castle tours. Sadly, our son was no better with money—the earning of it, I mean, not the spending of it. By the time Alejandro became duke, the roof of the castle was caving in, we were mortgaged to the hilt, and I was beginning to think I'd spend my elderly years begging on the streets, or selling oranges at street corners."

I laughed. "As if Alejandro would ever allow that." I smiled, remembering his bossy ways when he'd informed me that taking financial care of us was his job. "He, at least, had no trouble figuring out how to make money."

"No." She smiled, playing patty-cake with the baby. "But of course, his background is so different. He didn't have an overbearing father constantly telling him how an aristocrat was supposed to behave. The small silver lining of having no father at all, I suppose...."

"No father?" Frowning, I lifted the brush off the canvas. I looked around the easel. "But Alejandro's father was the duke. Your son."

Maurine looked up at me sharply, her face oddly pale. "Oh, yes. Of course."

I gave a laugh. "Is the sun getting to you, Maurine?"

"I'm an old woman. I get confused." Her blue eyes suddenly wouldn't meet mine. "But you're right. I think I've been in the sun too long."

She rose to her feet, still holding Miguel, who looked happy to be moving at last after so long sitting still. "I'm a little tired. I'll have the staff bring you some lemonade. And maybe look for Alejandro's hairbrush. Yes, his hairbrush..."

She left the rose garden without waiting for a

reply. I stared after her, frowning. What did lemonade have to do with Alejandro's hairbrush?

"I thought she would never leave."

With a gasp, I whirled around. The paintbrush fell from my limp hand, landing with a soft thud into the grass.

Edward St. Cyr stood in the rose garden, near the thick hedge on the edge of the forest. Brambles had ripped the sleeves of his dark tailored jacket.

"Edward," I breathed. "What are you doing here?"

He stopped five feet in front of me, looking down at me. His eyes were stark against his tanned face as he gazed at me hungrily. "You have no idea how I've wanted to see your face."

He reached out a hand, but I stumbled backward, my long skirt dragging against the grass. Holding my floppy pink hat against my head, I glanced uneasily to the left and right.

Having him here, in Maurine's rose garden—in Alejandro's castle—felt all kinds of wrong. Like finding a deadly snake amid the lush flowers. "How did you get in here?"

His lips twisted. "It wasn't easy."

"I told you I never wanted to see you again!"

I narrowed my eyes. "You must get out of here! Alejandro will kill you if he finds you here!"

"Ah, but he's gone, isn't he?"

I sucked in my breath.

"And as for your precious duke..." A low, guttural curse came from Edward's lips. "I know you don't want him." He looked contemptuously around the lush, sunlit garden, to the stone walls of the castle just beyond the perfectly trimmed green hedges. "I've come to save you from this... prison."

"It's not a prison," I retorted. "It's my home! And Alejandro is no jailer. I..." I licked my lips, then whispered aloud, "I love him."

Edward's eyes narrowed, and his lips twisted downward, giving him an expression that was hard, even cruel.

"He seduced you, didn't he?" He took another step toward me, and I again backed away, knocking over the easel behind me. I gulped as Edward slowly looked me over, from my hat to my long cotton skirt covered with an artist's long smock. "He's got to you." He straightened, and this time his contemptuous glance was just for me, all for me. "You fell for his lines *again*."

I took a deep breath.

"I love him," I said quietly. "In a way I never loved you—and I never will."

His hands tightened at his sides.

"The charming Duque de Alzacar. Beloved by all." His lip curled. "Of course you're faithful to him. But is he faithful to you?"

I drew myself up coldly. "Of course."

"Are you sure?" He lifted a dark eyebrow. "You know, you must know, about the woman he visits in Granada?"

My lips parted. "Woman?"

"Ah," Edward said, smiling. "You didn't know. They have dinner together. Often. He bought her a tavern in the Albaicín district. Sometimes he even plays his guitar there. Singing old Spanish love songs. In front of everyone."

My mouth went dry.

Alejandro hadn't played his guitar for me. Not once.

Licking my lips, I croaked, "There are all kinds of reasons for…"

Edward moved in for the kill. "Sometimes he stays the night in the residence above her tavern. But sometimes," he said softly, "he just goes for a quick visit. For the day." His lips curled. "A bit of love in the afternoon."

The chill turned to ice. I desperately tried to think of a reasonable explanation for why Alejandro hadn't wanted me to come with him today.

I'll come with you!

It will be a one-day trip, there and back. Very boring. Stay here with Miguel.

It was the nightmare I'd imagined when I'd refused to marry Alejandro. Except this was a million times worse.

Because I'd let myself love him.

"Lying to your face." Edward came closer. "He has no shame. He thinks, in his arrogance, that he can have you, as well. He's out enjoying himself—keeping you prisoner...."

"I'm not a prisoner," I choked out.

He lifted a condescending eyebrow. "No?" He slowly looked around the rose garden. "I could make him pay," he whispered. "I could make him regret."

I gasped—not in fear, but in fury. "If you dare hurt him, I'll..."

"*Hurt* him?" His blue eyes suddenly blazed. "*He* is the one you are worried about? Where was his concern for *you* when he left your heart in ashes?" He took another step toward me, his expression changing as he reached toward me almost wistfully. "Where is your love for me, for saving you…?"

I turned away, stepping back out of his reach. My voice was very cold. "I appreciated your friendship—until the moment I realized you had no time for my baby."

"Lena, you can't…"

"If you touch me, I'll scream. And Alejandro will come running…."

Edward moved closer.

"He's not here, though, is he?"

This time, the expression in his face scared me. For a moment, I stared at him, heart pounding. But as I opened my mouth to scream, like a miracle, I heard Alejandro's voice from the other side of the garden.

"Lena? Are you out here?"

I nearly wept with relief.

"I'm here!" I shouted. "I'm here, Alejandro! In the rose garden!"

Shaking, I turned back to face Edward, but he was already gone, melted back into the forest.

"And don't ever come back," I whispered aloud. I prayed I'd never see him again. But I still heard his ugly words.

You know, you must know, about the woman he visits in Granada?

He was *lying,* I told myself. Alejandro told me he'd be loyal, that he'd been faithful for the past year, wanting only me....

But then, I remembered, he'd also told me he was a liar.

When I saw my husband's strong, powerful body push through the trees to me, I nearly wept.

"Querida," Alejandro murmured, kissing my forehead as he pulled me into his arms. "I came back early. I couldn't bear to be away for...but what's this?" He drew back, his handsome face the picture of concern. "You're shaking."

"It's nothing," I said. My teeth chattered. "M-my easel fell."

"Ah." He smiled at me, his dark eyes warm. "Let me take care of that."

"Don't look at the painting!" I cried. "It's supposed to be a surprise. For your birthday."

Good-naturedly covering his eyes, he handed me the canvas. "I didn't see a thing."

I took the painting, slightly smeared from the fall and half-finished, with Maurine and Miguel looking like ghosts. And I wished I'd covered my ears and not heard a thing when Edward had told me about the woman in Granada.

"It has occurred to me," Alejandro murmured a week later, leaning over the sofa where I sat feeding Miguel, "that we never had a honeymoon."

"Honeymoon?" I said, twisting my head to look back at him. I shook my head. "You mean, without Miguel?"

"Don't worry." He brushed the back of my neck with his fingertips, making me shiver. "I'm not thinking Tahiti. That will have to wait. But a single night, just a two-hour drive away, surely you could manage that?"

I hesitated. "I don't know..."

"I promise you'll enjoy it." He stroked my hair, then gently kissed the crook of my neck, the edge between my shoulder and my neck. My shiver turned harder. "We will get a nice hotel. Go out for dinner. I'm thinking Granada...."

"Granada?" I stared at him, and the color must have drained from my cheeks, because he frowned.

"I thought you wanted to see the Alhambra."

I'd dreamed of seeing the famous Moorish castle since I was a child. But I'd spent the past week guarding my heart. Trying to stay distant and cold. Trying not to think about what I didn't want to know. Granada was the last place on earth I wanted to go.

Or was it?

"Maybe," I said.

He smiled, really smiled, for the first time in a week. Since I'd started keeping my distance, even when we were as close as a man and woman could be. "Is that a yes?" He tilted his head, looking over me slowly with a sensual, heavy-lidded gaze. "I'd be happy to spend time persuading you...."

My body immediately clamored for him to persuade me, hot and sweet and long. But sex wasn't our problem. We made love every night. Physically, we were closer than ever.

Emotionally, the weight of secrets had caused an ocean between us.

You know, you must know, about the woman he visits in Granada?

My smile faded. Like my courage. I shook my head. "On second thought...forget it."

"Why?" His eyes narrowed, and he moved around the sofa with lightning speed. He cupped my face, looking down at me fiercely. "I am trying to make it up to you!"

"What?" I breathed, searching his gaze. "What are you trying to make up for, Alejandro?"

"Whatever has made you so angry at me." His fingertips tightened infinitesimally. "I want you to look at me like you used to."

"And I want to trust you," I choked out, "like I used to."

He stared at me. He'd never heard that tone from me before. "When I was in Granada…"

I held my breath.

He continued, "You were alone with my grandmother. Did she…" He hesitated. "Did she say something?"

"Did she tell me your secret, you mean?" I said bitterly. "No. She is loyal to you."

He abruptly released me and rose from the sofa, his face hard. "Enough. We are taking a one-night honeymoon. You will come with me. You will have a good time."

I lifted my chin defiantly. "Is that a command, Your Excellency?"

"Take it as you wish." He glared back at me, his eyes cold. "I will tell the staff to pack your things immediately."

The drive to Granada was short, especially after Alejandro stepped on the gas of his yellow Lamborghini. But with just the two of us trapped in the small space, it still took far too long. The tension between us was boiling, about to explode.

I forced myself to look at the guidebook he'd bought me about Granada. I tried to distract myself with its history. To choke back my frustration, my hurt, my rage. Because if I let out my feelings, I feared our marriage would end, and so would any chance at happiness. Forever.

I desperately wanted to ask him about the woman.

I desperately was afraid of the answer.

Alejandro did not speak to me. He drove us to a small hotel, a *parador* amidst the gardens of the Alhambra itself, in a building that was once a fifteenth-century convent, and a royal chapel to the kings of Spain, and before that, a palace and mosque of the Moorish emirs. Once there, he seemed angry at everyone. He glowered at the hotel staff. The moment we were alone in the simple, starkly furnished bedroom, he turned on me, and pressed me to the large four-poster bed in a ruthless, unyielding embrace.

All the women's magazines tell you to do one thing. To have self-esteem. To turn away from any man you cannot completely trust. Especially one who has broken your heart before. They say the past predicts the future.

I knew all this, but when I felt his hand stroke my cheek, the sweet satin stroke of his touch sent liquid fire through my veins. I saw the dark gleam of his eyes as he slowly lowered his head to mine, and I could not resist.

He kissed me, and I felt my heart explode in my chest. Felt my taped-together soul shatter again into a million pieces, even tinier than before, in infinite chiming shards that I would never be able to put together again.

I had to ask him. I had to be brave enough to ask, and be brave enough to listen to his answer—whether he answered with words, or with silence.

I suddenly realized this might be the very last time we'd ever make love....

"Maravillosa," Alejandro whispered against my skin. As he pulled off my clothes, as I pulled off his, as I kissed him, tasting the salt of his skin, I knew that even amid the pleasure, I was tasting the salt of my own tears.

I loved him.

So much.

And I knew—I'd always known, really—how this would someday end.

Through my tears, I kissed him back desperately, letting him pull me into the whirlwind of mingled anguish and pleasure.

But when the heat between us was satisfied, coldness was all that was left. Both of us still naked, he held me against him on the bed. His voice was low.

"Why do you not look at me like you used to? What has changed? What do you—know?"

I looked at him. His face shimmered through my tears.

"Edward came to see me last week. At Rohares."

"What!" he exploded, sitting up.

I held his hand. "I didn't ask him to come. He snuck in. I only spoke with him for a moment. He wanted me to run away with him. When I refused, he told me…you had a woman here. In Granada. That you visited her. That you bought her a tavern. That you even sing to her…."

For a long moment, we stared at each other in the slanted bars of sunlight coming through the window blinds. I could almost hear the pounding of my heart.

Then Alejandro's lip slowly curled.

"I will kill him," he said, and with cold menace, started to rise from the bed.

"No!" Grabbing his arm, I looked up at him pleadingly. "It's not about Edward anymore. It's about us. You and me." I swallowed, blinking fast as I whispered, "Do you love her?"

He looked down at me.

"Yes," he said dully.

My lips parted in a silent, heartsick gasp. Numbly, I let him go.

"So that is your big secret. The thing I expected from the beginning." I tried to laugh, wiping my eyes. "How very boring."

"It's not like that." Sitting on the edge of the bed, he scowled at me. "You think so little of my loyalty, even after all the time we've spent together?"

"But you said you love her," I whispered. "You've never said that to me. Not once."

I heard his intake of breath. "It's not like that," he repeated, setting his jaw. "Theresa is not my mistress."

"Then what?" I choked out. "What secret could you possibly be keeping, that would hurt me worse than that?"

"I protect the people I love. At any cost." His voice was bleak. I looked at him sharply, and saw the vulnerability in his eyes. The yearning. He took a deep, shuddering breath. "How I wish I could tell you everything."

Our eyes locked. Held. I opened my lips to plead—

He shook his head and rose to his feet. The yearning in his expression shuttered. His face returned to the handsome mask I knew so well—powerful, ruthless and cold.

"Come," he said. "Our time is short."

After a silent luncheon on the lovely terrace of the *parador,* we walked through the gardens of the Alhambra, with their flowers and trees and wide lush pools. As beautiful and varied and wide as they were, they didn't hold a candle to the gardens of Rohares, in my opinion. Though perhaps I was biased. Because the castle had become my home.

Alejandro held my hand tightly as we walked. I didn't even try to resist. The truth was I wanted the comfort of his hand. It felt warm and strong in mine. Was it wrong of me to still want to believe? To trust him?

Yes. I was a fool. Any of the women's magazines would have called me an idiot for not already being on my way to a lawyer's office. And yet...

We met a guide who took us on a private tour.

We walked through the graceful arcades of the Alhambra complex, through the lush terraces with their views of Granada in the valley below, past the blue pools hedged by myrtle, reflecting the wide blue sky. But in spite of the fact that I'd dreamed of visiting the Alhambra all my life, I barely noticed the beauty. As we walked through cavernous rooms, decorated with tile and geometric patterns and arabesques of Arabic calligraphy in plaster, beneath jaw-dropping ceilings soaring high above, of the sun and stars, my mind was scrambling, trying to put the clues together.

Why would Alejandro need to protect Maurine and Miguel? What could the secret be?

We had our picture taken together in the famous stone Court of the Lions, from the fourteenth century.

"No," the guide laughed. "You are newlyweds. Stand closer."

And so Alejandro put his arm around me. I looked up at his face, and again, I saw the yearning in his eyes. The yearning that matched my own.

"*¡Perfecto!* Now you look like lovers!"

As we left the Alhambra, I turned back to look at it one last time. It had been neglected over the years, vandalized, nearly blown up by Napoleon's soldiers. But after all that, it stood tall and proud over Granada. Unbowed. Unbroken. And so beautiful now. So loved.

"We don't need to see any more," I whispered over the ache in my throat.

"You're here. See it all." Silently, Alejandro drove us down the mountain to the city. We visited the Capilla Real, the royal chapel, getting special permission for a private tour that took us immediately past the long line of tourists outside, past the gypsies begging on the streets and musicians busking along the crowded edges.

In the dark, quiet interior of the enormous stone chapel, I saw the tomb of Ferdinand and Isabella, who together had practically ruled the medieval world in their day, even before they'd sent Columbus in ships to the New World. Together, they'd finally ended seven hundred years of Moorish rule, laying siege to Granada and driving the last sultan, called Boabdil, from the city.

It was said that the reason he gave up without a fight was to prevent the destruction of his beloved Alhambra. And so he spent the rest of his life mocked, and in poverty, a sultan without a throne....

Alejandro came to stand beside me in the cool shadows of the royal crypt. "What are you thinking?"

I looked at him. "How loving the wrong thing—or the wrong person—can ruin your life," I whispered.

"Sí," he said quietly. He turned away. "Come. This place leaves me cold."

Outside the echoes of the shadow-filled chapel, we were hit by the brilliant Spanish sunlight, the noise of tourists laughing and talking, the distant sound of music. Life.

"Enough history," Alejandro said, shaking his head ruefully. "There's an ice-cream shop down the street, the most famous in Granada. The American first lady visited here recently and said it was the best ice cream in all of Spain...."

But I wasn't listening. I was too busy trying to think things through. Eating the ice-cream cone some time later as we walked, I looked at Alejandro sideways beneath my lashes. He was so handsome, so dark-haired and broad-shouldered. The man of my dreams, come to life.

What was the secret? What was it he couldn't tell me, for fear of endangering his grandmother and his son?

We walked through the narrow streets of Granada, and I bought some chocolates and a garden ornament for Maurine, and a small stuffed toy for Miguel, plus a wooden sword and shield he wouldn't be able to play with for at least a year.

I couldn't stop thinking of that last sultan, Boabdil, who'd sacrificed everything, his honor, his fortune, his pride, rather than see the palace he loved blown up into ash.

What would I sacrifice for love?

What would you?

Love me? Alejandro's words floated back to me. *You do not even know me.*

Maybe he'd been right. A year ago, maybe I'd just fallen for his power, his wealth, his influence. His beauty.

But now, as I looked at his face, I loved him for who he really was. The man who took care of everyone. Who was willing to sacrifice himself for those he cared about. As a father. A grandson. A neighbor. A boss.

A husband.

My heart caught in my chest. What was I missing?

Twilight was falling when Alejandro suggested

we go out for dinner and drinks. "A…friend of mine owns a restaurant in the Albaicín district."

I looked at him sharply. He nodded.

"Yes," he said quietly, watching me in the deepening dusk. "I want you to meet her."

I was shaking when we walked up the cobblestoned alleys of the Albaicín, the old Moorish quarter on the hillside beneath the Alhambra. We reached a prosperous-looking tavern, filled with people and music. I froze.

"Come on," Alejandro said gently. "It'll be all right." Pulling me inside, he brought me through the crowds to the bar, where he was greeted eagerly by the other patrons.

"Are you going to play tonight, *señor?*"

With a slight smile, he shook his head. "Where is Theresa?"

The man motioned toward the end of the bar with his glass of sangria. With a quick nod, Alejandro pulled me down toward a dark-haired woman.

"Theresa," he said, kissing her on each cheek.

"Alejandro," she exclaimed, returning the embrace. "I didn't expect you so soon!"

I stared at the woman. She wasn't what I'd expected. She had dark eyes and a round, friendly

252 UNCOVERING HER NINE MONTH SECRET

face, and she seemed at least ten years older than Alejandro. She smiled as she turned to me. "And this must be your wife." A big smile lit up her face. "Your Lena?"

My lips parted. *His* Lena?

"Sí." Alejandro put his arm around me. "My Lena."

"I'm so happy to meet you at last!" she said with clear delight. "I told him he had to bring you here. Wait until you hear him play!"

"Play?" I echoed, looking at him.

He blushed. I swear he did. "Yes. I play a little guitar sometimes. No one cares I'm a duke here. They only care how well I play the guitar...."

"Are you that good?"

"Let him show you." Theresa gave me a wink. "Drink orders always go up thirty percent when you sing, Alejandro." She turned to me with a smile. "Go grab a table, if you can find one.... And what will you have?"

"Bourbon," he said. "Rocks."

"Right. Lena?"

"Something light...sangria?"

She chuckled. "Light?"

"Isn't it mostly juice with a bit of red wine?"

She gave a hearty guffaw and glanced at Alejandro affectionately. "Innocent little thing, isn't she?"

"Very," he said quietly.

She sighed, looking back at me, she suggested, "I'll make you a *tinto de verano*. Dash of wine, sugar and a little lime with sparkling water. Trust me. It won't go to your head."

She was right. The delicious concoction was a mixture of tart and sweet and bubbles, with lemon and limes floating beside the ice. I had one glass, then another, then a third, then looked down at my empty plate and realized I'd ordered and eaten a whole plate of dinner without paying the slightest attention.

"What time is it?" My head was swimming. I put my hands to my temples. "She said this drink wouldn't go to my head," I said accusingly.

Alejandro gave a low laugh. "It wouldn't, but you had four of them."

"Four?" I looked with amazement at my empty glass. "They just taste so light. The most delicious wine cooler ever invented."

"You should stop."

I looked at him brazenly. "You should tell me who you really are."

Time suddenly stood still.

"Don't you know?" he said hoarsely. "Haven't you guessed?"

"Don't tell me you're already having your first fight." Theresa was holding out a guitar. "Fix it, *pequeño*. Play."

"Sí!" the people around us clamored, pounding on their tables. "Play!"

Alejandro shook his head. "We're leaving."

But I didn't want to leave. I wanted to see what everyone else apparently already knew. The other side of my husband. The one he'd never let me see. "Will you play?" I whispered. "For me?"

He whirled to look at me. Then he gave a slow nod. "For you, *mi amor*." He slowly took the guitar in his hand, and there was a burst of cheers and applause. "This is just for you."

Walking across the crowded tavern, past all the tables to the tiny stage, Alejandro sat on a stool. With his guitar in his lap, he said simply into the microphone, "This is for my bride. The mother of my child." He looked at me. "The woman I love."

My lips parted in a silent gasp.

Could he have said…

Surely he couldn't have said…

How strong were those *tinto de verano* drinks anyway?

Exhaling, Alejandro strummed his guitar, and in a low, husky voice began to sing. It sounded very old, and Spanish. He was a good musician, I thought in amazement, really good, far better than any tycoon-slash-duke had a right to be. The music was so heartbreaking and pure that at first, I didn't bother to listen to the words.

Then I did.

Alejandro stared at me from across the room, and sang about a young peasant boy who'd dared to put on the clothes of a prince. He'd gone through life as an imposter, until he died heart-broken, wishing he could see, just one last time, the peasant girl he'd left behind.

Love me? My whole body flashed hot, then cold as his words took on new significance. *You do not even know me.*

I dimly heard the whispers hissing through the room. "That's the Duke of Alzacar—and she must be his new wife—they're obviously in love…."

But I just listened to the music, and suddenly, it all fell into place.

Maurine's shaky words. *If not for him, I never would have survived the aftermath of that car crash, when I lost my whole family…. I can still see him in the hospital, his little injured face cov-*

ered with bandages, his eyes so bright.... He was worried about me, not himself. "It'll be all right, Abuela," he told me. "I'm your family now."

Pilar's voice. *I know it was always your desire to have a larger family, growing up so lonely, up in that huge castle, with your older sister off working in Granada. And your mother working night and day, when she wasn't distracted by the duke....*

I couldn't breathe. I felt as if I was choking. The walls of the tavern were pressing in. Rising unsteadily to my feet, I pushed through the tables and headed for the door. I saw Theresa's surprised face as I flung it open and headed outside.

In the quiet night, in the empty, cobblestoned alley, I fell back against the rough stone wall and looked up at the moonlight, shaking. I jumped when I heard the slam of the door behind me.

"So now you understand," Alejandro said quietly behind me.

"You're not the duke at all," I choked out, hardly able to believe it even as I said it. "The real Alejandro died in that crash, didn't he? Along with his parents. And your mother—the housekeeper."

"I had to do it." The only sign of emotion was the slight tightening of his jaw, the low tone of his voice. "Maurine had lost everything. And I loved her. Growing up in the castle, she'd always treated me like a grandson. And on that terrible day, the day of the crash, she lost everyone. When she came to see me at the hospital, she seemed to have aged ten years. She was so alone. I couldn't leave her to die in the dilapidated castle, with no one to take care of her...." Swallowing, he looked down at the cobblestoned street. Moonlight left a trail of silver on his dark silhouette as he said quietly, "So I told Maurine I would be her family from now on. Her grandson."

"How is it possible no one knew?"

"Alejandro and I looked very much alike. We were the same age, same build. And after the accident, my face was injured. We used that to explain the difference. Not that anyone asked. People had long since stopped coming to the castle. The duke and his family had chased most of the tenants away by harassing them over rents. Even their old society friends shunned them, since they were always asking to borrow money. Alejandro's parents felt ashamed of how far they'd fallen. Just not ashamed enough to work for something better." He looked up. "My mother was the only servant left, and she hadn't been paid in a year." Taking a deep breath, he said simply, "When Abuela claimed I was her grandson, and pawned the last of her jewelry to pay the transfer-of-title fees, no one questioned it."

"But a few people knew."

He nodded. "Pilar, our governess." He glanced at the restaurant door. "My older sister. Theresa."

My lips parted. "Your sister?"

"Half sister. She's eight years older. She was working in Granada when the accident happened. She rushed to the hospital as soon as she heard, but Abuela convinced her to keep the secret. They have all kept it. Because they love me. And they love Abuela." He looked away. "As I grew older, it felt wrong, stealing Alejandro's title and name. I promised myself that I would never marry, never have a child. The family line, and the family lie, would end with me. I convinced myself that was redemption."

I stared at him, tears now falling down my cheeks in the moonlight. "That was why you said you're no good at keeping promises," I whispered. "Because you had a child. And then you married me. I thought…" I shook my head. "I thought you meant you could never keep your promises of fidelity…."

"That I would cheat on you?" he said incredulously. He came closer, his face blazing with emotion as he reached out to cup my cheek. "From the moment we met, you've been the only woman I wanted. Even for the year we were apart—there was no one else for me. No one."

"But…when I told you I loved you…"

He gave a low, humorless laugh. He shook his head. "You really don't understand, do you? When I promised myself I'd never marry or have a child, I made sure I would keep that promise by only allowing myself to date women like Claudie… cold, sophisticated, heartless women I'd never be tempted to love. You were different. You were the woman I could not resist," he said softly. "You made me break every promise I'd made to myself. I wanted to tell you everything. Where you were concerned, I had no self-control."

I stared up at him, my lips parted.

"When I heard you were pregnant with my child, I was desperate to find you. But once I did, and we were wed, I suddenly knew I'd never be able to tell you the truth. At first, because I was afraid you'd use the information to blackmail me, and try to take my son away. Then because

I owed it to Miguel. You were so proud our son would someday be a duke...."

"I never cared about that!" I said fiercely. "All I care about is you. And Miguel..." I looked up at him with an intake of breath. "Your real name is Miguel."

He gave me a wicked grin. "You can see why I didn't mind our son's name."

My knees shook, because my world was spinning. "But after we were married—surely then you knew you could trust me?"

"You have such an honest heart." He sobered. "I didn't want you to have the burden."

"Burden? Are you kidding?" I gave a laugh that was giddy, almost hysterical. "If you knew what I'd imagined..."

"It's worse than you think." His face had turned deadly serious. "My grandmother and I both broke laws with our lies. We could be charged with fraud and possibly sent to prison. For myself, I would have been willing to take the risk, to tell you the truth. But Maurine..." He looked down. "I was afraid to take the risk, for her sake. The idea of her in jail..."

A sudden noise down the quiet street, perhaps

a cat knocking over a trash can in a nearby alley, caused us both to jump. I looked at him.

"You can trust me. No one will ever know." I swallowed and whispered. "Did you really mean what you said in the tavern?"

"The song?"

"That you—" I blushed a little "—actually—love me?"

His eyes went wide. Then, with a low laugh, he pulled me in his arms.

"Oh, *querida.* I have loved you from almost the first moment we met. Your sweetness, your nobility, your honesty."

"I was so afraid.... I believed all the wrong things...."

Alejandro wrapped his hands around mine. "And now you hold my heart, my life, in your hands," he said quietly. "You have the power to take Miguel from me, to go back to Mexico, to walk away." He lifted his dark gaze to mine in the moonlight. "You own me completely. What will you do?"

"What will I do?" I whispered, tears in my eyes. Putting my arms around him, I pulled him close and pressed my forehead against his heart. "I will love you, Alejandro. Forever."

CHAPTER TEN

WE ROSE FOR a late breakfast the next morning, after a night in our hotel room with much giggling and even more lovemaking. As eager as I was to see our baby after a whole night away from him, I was also lingering, enjoying every last moment of this brief, perfect honeymoon.

No one would ever be able to part us again.

"I think," Alejandro said thoughtfully as we left the hotel, "that was the best honeymoon I've ever had."

"Best and only," I said.

"No, surely not only. Our marriage will be nothing but one long honeymoon," he said huskily, then to prove it, he kissed me. The kiss soon became so intense and deep that Alejandro muttered something about renting the room for another night, and started to pull me back toward the hotel.

"But we can't!" I protested with a laugh. "Miguel…"

"All right," he grumbled, then his eyes smoldered. "But I'm taking you back to our bedroom as fast as the car will go."

But at my request, we returned to Rohares the long way. He took me to the spot where legend said Boabdil, the last sultan of Spain, took his very last look at Granada, after he was forced to cede it to Spanish King Ferdinand and Queen Isabella.

"Oh, no. I left the guidebook at the hotel," I said sadly, then brightened. "But I left my name in it. Hopefully they'll find it and call."

"A guidebook? Get another one!"

"It's a souvenir," I whispered, "of the happiest night of my life."

He kissed me, then standing on the hill, we looked back at Granada. "They say Boabdil wept when he looked his last upon his city," I said wistfully. "And his mother mocked his tears. She sneered that he was weeping like a woman for what he could not fight for as a man. Can you believe that?"

"People can say hurtful things to those they love," Alejandro said quietly. "Especially when they're backed into a corner and their own hearts are breaking."

As we drove back home, I suddenly realized

Alejandro was right. I thought of all my anguished years feeling lonely in London, wishing hopelessly for my grandmother, my uncle and Claudie to love me. But they could not, because they did not know how. Instead, they'd relentlessly pursued the wrong things, luxury and status and appearance. They'd never known that the only way to gain happiness was not only to follow your heart, but to give it away.

Leaning over, Alejandro took my hand. Bringing it to his lips, he fervently kissed it. My eyes blurred with tears as I smiled at him, thinking how lucky I was.

And that was the moment I forgave my family for not loving me. Sometimes, I thought, you have to make your own family.

Blushing, I said shyly, "So what do I call you now?"

He looked at me. "I've grown fond of Alejandro. I'll let my son keep Miguel." He turned away, facing the road. His hands tightened on the steering wheel. "After we get back, I'm going to talk to a lawyer. I'll see if there's any way to renounce the title without causing risk to Maurine." He looked at me. "But it seems so much to ask of you."

"What?"

"Would you be heartbroken to give up the title of duchess—and know Miguel would never be a duke?"

"Are you kidding?" I gave a low laugh. "I'm happy to give it up. Do you really think I'm duchess material?"

He looked at me seriously. "Yes, *mi amor*. Yes."

"I'm happy as your wife," I whispered. "However that may be." And he squeezed my hand in his.

When we arrived at Rohares Castle, we hugged our baby and Maurine, who immediately started telling us every small detail of their extremely uneventful night, which mostly involved patty-cake and Miguel dozing as his great-grandmother read him Washington Irving's *Tales of the Alhambra*. "So Miguel felt part of the experience, too. It seemed appropriate...."

"Like his name," I said. Smiling, I glanced back at Alejandro. "It turns out I named him after his father."

With an intake of breath, Maurine looked between us. Then she gave a whoop of joy. "Took you long enough," she cried, then hugged us, telling us we were silly to be so emotional as she wiped her own eyes. "So. I, too, have news. The best news of all." Maurine looked between us, beaming. "While the two of you were on your honeymoon, I did something with your hairbrush...."

The house phone rang loudly from across the great room. Wondering if it might be the hotel calling about my guidebook, I said hurriedly, "Just a minute." Rushing across the room, I answered breathlessly, "Hello?"

"Don't say my name."

Edward?! I gritted my teeth and rasped, "I'm hanging up now."

"If you do, you'll be sorry."

Something about the cool confidence of his voice made me hesitate. "Why?"

"Because I know."

"What?"

"Everything."

A chill went down my spine. I tried to bluff. "Everything about what?"

"About your husband. And the lie he told twenty-three years ago."

The chill turned to ice. "I don't know what you're talking about."

He snorted, then said quietly, "I followed you to Granada. I was in the shadows on the street.

When you came out alone from the restaurant, I was going to comfort you. Then your husband followed you out. And gave me all the ammunition I would ever need to destroy him. And that so-called grandmother of his."

Turning, I stared wide-eyed at Alejandro and Maurine across the great hall, where they were laughing together. I gripped the phone. "What do you want?"

"What I've always wanted. You."

"I don't love you—"

"Yes. I know. You love him. So if you want to protect him, this choice should be easy for you. I'm waiting in a car at the castle gate. Call the guard. Tell him to let me in."

"If I tell Alejandro how you're trying to blackmail me, he will kill you."

"I'm sure you're right. Which is why you won't tell him."

"You don't understand! That's not just an expression. He will literally kill you!"

"Let him try," he said flatly. "Tell him, if that's how you want this to go. I'm not afraid. I have nothing to lose." He paused. "Do you?"

I shuddered, trembling, afraid that Alejandro would really kill him, and he'd end up in jail not just for fraud, but for murder. "What do you want me to do?"

His voice was smooth and slick. "Tell him you've changed your mind about your marriage. Tell him you only wanted him when you thought he was a real duke, but now...you're in love with me."

Horror filled my heart. "He'll never believe it—"

"He *will*. That's what frightens you." He gave a low laugh. "Tell him you're going to spend tonight with me, and your lawyers will be in touch about divorce—and custody. That bit about custody is just for you, by the way. I'll let your baby live with us. Doesn't that show how much I care?"

"You never cared about me," I whispered. "If you did, you couldn't do this."

"I took care of you. I saved you. I earned you. Not him."

"I'm a human soul—not some trophy to be won!"

"You should be mine," he said coldly. "Let him watch you leave with me. Make him believe I'm the one you want. And I'll forget what I know. Do it for his sake. And the old woman's."

"Edward, please..."

"Three minutes. Then I'm calling a press conference."

"And he'll kill you!"

"Then Navaro will be in jail for the rest of his life. And your kid will have no father. Or great-grandmother. Make your choice. You say you really love them? Prove it."

The line clicked off.

My whole body shook as I hung up.

"Who was it?" Alejandro said behind me.

"N-nothing. I mean, no one."

"Which is it? Is something wrong?" His eyes were sharp. Of course he knew something was wrong. He saw right through me. Saw my anguished heart.

So how could I break his—with a lie?

And yet—how could I not?

Wide-eyed, I looked across the great hall toward Maurine, who at her age would likely never come back from the shock of a scandal and trial for fraud, much less being sent to prison. I looked at my sweet baby in his baby swing, who would endure the experience I'd feared most—being surrounded by paparazzi—before he lost his father. And Alejandro. I looked at him, hardly able to breathe. If he really did attack Edward as I feared…

I remembered the look in his eyes in Granada when I'd told him that Edward had visited me. I remembered the cold menace in his face.

I will kill him.

"Lena?" Alejandro frowned, coming closer. "Who was on the phone?"

The phone suddenly rang again. I picked it up.

"Your Excellency?" It was the security guard at the gate. "There's an Edward St. Cyr here. He has no appointment. Should I let him inside?"

I took a deep breath.

"Let him in," I said faintly, then hung up the phone. I picked up my handbag. I walked slowly toward my family, feeling as if I was going to die.

But I would die for them. I looked at those three beloved faces, in this beautiful old castle I'd already come to love. My family. My home. Would I do it? To save them?

Yes.

"Where are you going?" Alejandro said.

"I'm sorry." My teeth were chattering. My words were faint. "Our marriage is over. I'll be back tomorrow. So we can discuss c-custody…."

I stopped at the door. Alejandro was staring at

me with open-mouthed shock. I was trembling so hard it was all I could do not to black out.

But it was the only way to save him. To save all of them.

I was the one who'd allowed Edward into our lives. I was the one who should pay for that. Not them.

But as I looked into Alejandro's face, I knew that he, too, would suffer. Squeezing my eyes shut, I turned away.

"Edward's come for me," I choked out. "I'm leaving with him now. We both know it never would have worked out with us, Alejandro. Not for long..."

"What are you saying?" he breathed, searching my gaze. "I don't believe you!"

"I'll be back with a lawyer—tomorrow...." My voice ended on a sob. Whirling around, I fled for the door. Outside, I saw Edward waiting in an expensive SUV. The windows were all rolled down, the engine still running. Sobbing, I climbed in beside him. He gave me a triumphant, cruel smile.

"Wise choice," he said coldly. "Very smart."

"I don't feel smart," I whispered, hating myself, hating this choice already, wanting to do nothing more than jump out of the vehicle. And suddenly, that's just what I needed to do. "No. NO. I can't do this—"

Reaching over me, Edward put on my seat belt. It felt like a restraint.

"You'll soon be free of his influence," he said softly, reaching toward me. "I promise you."

I shuddered at his touch. "Don't!"

With a low laugh, he put down his hand. "Have it your way. I am a patient man...."

But as he turned the steering wheel and started to drive down the circular courtyard, Alejandro was suddenly there, standing ahead of us, blocking the way to the road.

He wasn't looking at Edward. He was looking only at me. I saw his lips form my name.

"Make him believe you love me," Edward growled in a low voice. "Make him believe."

I licked my lips. I looked at Alejandro's stark face. The anguish in his dark eyes.

And I couldn't go through with it.

"I can't." My voice trembled as I started fumbling with my seat belt. "I can't do this. Let me out of here!"

"Too late," Edward said grimly, holding on to the latch as I tried to fight him.

Alejandro saw us struggling through the front

window. Hands clenched at his sides, he started walking toward the SUV, now staring at Edward with narrowed eyes, his powerful warrior's body threatening his murder.

Edward's mouth twisted as their eyes met. He glared back, the same expression of murder in his face.

They both intended to kill or be killed today.

Over me.

With a low, cruel growl, Edward stomped on the gas, increasing speed as he drove the SUV straight at Alejandro, who was unprotected and alone in the castle courtyard.

But my husband didn't turn and run. He didn't back down. Instead, he started running straight at the car—as if a man could play chicken against seven thousand pounds of steel!

I screamed. Grabbing the steering wheel, I twisted it hard to the left. Veering off balance, Edward's SUV crashed into the stone fountain and twisted, then flew, high into the air.

As if in slow motion, I felt us fly up, up, up, at the same time we flipped in sickening circles, around and around. We hit the ground with a bone-jarring crunch and rolled down the long hill, all the way down. Then, with a shudder and metallic groan, the SUV was still.

I wasn't dead. I was upside down, held into the passenger seat by the taut seat belt that had knocked the air out of me, leaving a streak of pain where it crossed my chest.

Panting, I looked over at the driver's seat. It was empty. Edward was gone.

"Lena!" Alejandro cried. A moment later, my door was wrenched open, and suddenly he was there. He yanked open the seat belt, and caught me in his strong arms as I fell.

Cradling me desperately, my husband sank to the ground, still holding me against his chest. He ran his hands over my body, found no life-ending injury and exhaled, holding me tight against him, rocking me in his lap. "Oh, my love," he choked out. "You're safe. You're safe. For a moment I thought…" He looked at me fiercely. "Don't ever do that to me again!"

"I'm sorry," I wept, pressing my head against his chest. "He learned the truth and said if I didn't come with him, he would ruin your life and Maurine's and even Miguel's. I couldn't risk you going to jail for the rest of your life—"

"I'd rather be sent to jail for a million years,"

he said hoarsely, "than lose you." I felt his body trembling beneath me. Reaching up in amazement, I brushed away a single tear trailing down his tanned, hard-edged cheek.

Pressing my forehead to his, I whispered, "Thank you for not letting me go."

He cupped my face, looked me straight in the eyes. "Never. We are forever...."

A low growl made us both turn.

"You'll be sorry." We turned to see Edward collapsed on the grass, where he'd been flung from the vehicle, across the hill. "Both of you," he panted, "will be sorry."

Alejandro's hands tightened on me. I looked up at him in terror. "Don't kill him. It's not worth it. Remember you promised you'd never leave me...."

"Kill him?" He looked at me incredulously. "Why should I? Look at him...."

For the first time, I noticed the odd way Edward's arms and legs were stretched out in unnatural directions on the grass. But even his body wasn't as contorted as his face.

"I'll tell the world," Edward panted, "how you all committed fraud. I'll ruin your lives—both of you—the old woman and that baby, too...."

Alejandro glared at Edward, parting his lips to answer. But someone else beat him to it.

"Calm down, dear. You're acting crazy."

Maurine stepped calmly between us on the hill. She peered down at Edward benignly, as if about to offer him cookies at a party, and the upside-down SUV behind us, with its crushed steel doors and a wheel still spinning, was just a decoration, like fairy lights or balloons. "Whatever you think is wrong, Alejandro is my grandson."

Edward gave a hard laugh. "It's a lie." He coughed. "I'll prove it when I get the court order for a blood test...."

"You know, I always wondered." She smiled, then looked at Alejandro, who was still on the ground, holding me protectively in his lap. She gave a brisk nod. "I was about to tell you, before all the fuss broke out. The hairbrush. You're my grandson, Alejandro. Really and truly. The grandson of my heart." She gave us a broad, self-satisfied smile. "Also a grandson of a DNA test."

I felt Alejandro jump. His face was pale.

"What...?" he breathed.

"The silly secret was just causing such a problem between you two." She looked between us severely. "And the way you were botching things. It just was ridiculous. Honestly, I'd always wondered why your mother stayed on as housekeeper for all those years, even when my son wasn't paying her. And then there was that family resemblance…. Anyway. It never mattered to me one way or the other. Until it started to interfere with your happiness." She grinned. "So I took your hairbrush and had a DNA test. You are my grandson, Alejandro. By heart, as you always were. But also by blood."

"No!" Edward screamed. Then he was suddenly quiet. I think he had fainted from pain.

Rather vengefully, I hoped he had. Although I didn't want him to die, of course. I didn't. Really, I didn't.

Alejandro's eyes were wide. "Is this true, Abuela?"

She nodded. "Remain the Duke of Alzacar, and if anyone wants to check if you are my grandson, let them." She looked at him and said quietly, "There is no one left in the family to inherit, if not you. No one you're cheating of his rightful due. And let me tell you something more. You're the finest duke of them all."

I saw him blinking suspiciously fast. He rose to his feet, helping me to rise, as well. He hugged his grandmother, then pulled me into the embrace.

When we finally pulled away, I wiped my eyes, then glanced over at Edward, still unconscious.

"We should call an ambulance, do you think?"

"I can see him breathing," Maurine said with a dismissive wave of her hand. "He's fine." She sighed. "But I'll call." She glanced at Alejandro. "And I expect the *policía* will want to come, as well...."

She went toward the castle, and Alejandro looked at me.

"She's right. We have only a few moments before the police arrive," he said quietly. "A choice must be made."

"So make it," I said, trusting whatever he'd decide.

He clawed back his hair. "I am tired of secrets. Tired of lies." He turned to me. "I never want another secret to shadow the light between us."

I nodded, unable to speak over the lump in my throat.

"So." He smiled at me, blinking fast, then gave a decisive nod. He walked over to Edward, who was still unconscious, his legs stretched out at a painful angle. He put his fingertips to the other man's neck, then straightened.

"Is he—dead?" I said. Not hopefully. Really.

He shook his head. "His pulse is strong. He will recover."

"Too bad," I said.

Alejandro looked at me in amazement. Coming back, he wrapped his arms around me. "It's not like you to be bloodthirsty, *mi amor,*" he murmured.

"I can be dangerous—" I reached up my hand to caress his cheek "—when it comes to protecting those I love."

"Yes." The corners of his sensual mouth quirked. Then his expression became serious. "But are you brave enough to face what lies ahead? There will be scandal. Or worse. Though perhaps I can protect Maurine…."

"How?"

"I will say that she was distraught over her family's death, and that I tricked her into believing I was her grandson."

"Oh, she won't like that at all."

"No," he agreed. He looked at me, emotion in his dark eyes. "Can you bear it, Lena? The storm that might come? Miguel will lose his legacy…."

"You're wrong." I put my hand on his cheek. My eyes were watery. "His legacy is more than some title. It's doing the right thing, even when it's hard."

"And love," Alejandro whispered, pressing my hands together as he kissed them fervently. "Loving for all your life, with all your heart."

"It's family, always and forever." Looking up at my husband, I smiled through my tears. "And whatever may come—our forever has already begun."

There are all kinds of ways to make a family.

Some ways are big, such as the way Maurine took in an orphaned twelve-year-old boy and insisted on claiming him as her grandson.

Some ways are small, such as when I sent an invitation to my wedding reception to my cousin Claudie.

Autumn had arrived at Rohares Castle, and with it harvest season for our tenants. The summer heat had subsided, leaving a gorgeous swath of vivid colors, of morning mists and early twilight, full of excuses to sip oceans of hot tea with milk in the morning and go to bed early with my husband with a bottle of ruby-red wine. Every night, we lit a fire in the fireplace—and in our bed. And that fire, as months passed, seemed only to get bigger and brighter.

Just that morning, Maurine had caught us kissing in the breakfast room. She'd laughed. "I don't think the honeymoon will really ever end for you two," she said affectionately. Then the doorbell rang, and she'd hurried from the room with a desperate cry: "The florist! Finally!" And we were alone.

I'd given Alejandro a sensual smile.

"Could I interest you in a little more honeymoon?" I said, batting my eyes coyly, to which my husband whispered, "All day, every day," before he kissed me senseless, then picked me up like a Neanderthal and carried me upstairs, back to bed.

Now, the crowded banqueting hall was lit up for evening, bedecked gloriously in autumn flowers in the most beautiful wedding reception I'd ever imagined. Across the crowds of our guests, I caught Alejandro's eye. He smiled back at me hungrily, as if it had been a year since he'd last taken me to bed, instead of just a few hours. His hot glance almost made me forget we were surrounded by family and friends.

"I told you he would be your husband," a voice crowed behind me. "I always can tell!"

"You were right." Turning, I smiled at Dolores, my neighbor from San Miguel de Allende who'd been whisked here from Mexico for the reception. She'd been equal parts impressed and triumphant when Alejandro had sent a private jet to collect her.

I'd sent Mr. Corgan, Mrs. Morris and Hildy a first-class ticket here from London. They were still working for Claudie. "But she's mellowed a great deal since she became Mrs. Crosby," the butler informed me. "He's rich, and that has made her very happy."

But I could see that for myself. Claudie had arrived at my door swathed in fur, with her brand-new husband at her side.

"I'm going to give you your inheritance back," was the first thing she announced to me. "David said it's the right thing to do. And besides—" she grinned "—we can afford it."

Same old Claudie, I thought. And yet not exactly the same. "Thank you," I said in surprise. I paused, then smiled. "Donate it to charity. Introduce me to your husband?"

She beamed. "I'd love to."

David Crosby was fat, short and bald, but he was indeed very rich, a king of Wall Street. They looked totally wrong together. Until you saw the way they looked at each other.

Claudie told me they'd met through a match-making service just for rich people.

"Trophy wives for billionaires?" I guessed.

"After all, Lena," she sniffed, "not everyone can manage to randomly fall pregnant by the love of their lives."

"No, indeed," I said.

"And I'm so happy..." she said wistfully, and I thought that she, too, must have been very lonely in London.

"I'm happy for you, truly," I said, and impulsively hugged her. My cousin stiffened, then let me hug her. I was encouraged. We weren't exactly best friends, but it was a start. And after all, we *were* family....

Pulling away, she wiped her eyes. "At least you dress better now. Your style used to make me physically ill."

Distant family, thankfully.

But Alejandro and I were surrounded by people who cared about us. I looked around at all the people who were here, celebrating our marriage. Thinking with relief about the one who was not.

I still woke up in a cold sweat occasionally,

thinking how I'd almost lost everything by getting into Edward St. Cyr's SUV that day.

Edward, sadly, had lived.

Oops, did I say that out loud?

Yes, he lived. From what I'd heard, he'd had an easier time than he deserved. A punctured lung and five broken bones. When the ambulance and police arrived, he'd refused to press charges against anyone, or even talk about the accident. But as he'd been lifted into the ambulance, our eyes had met, and he'd coldly and silently turned his face to the wall. He was done with me. A fact that left me profoundly grateful.

I tried to wish him well, because he had once been my friend.

Okay, but seriously. He'd tried to run over my husband with his Range Rover. That's not the kind of thing I could ever forgive, or forget. So mostly I just tried not to think of it.

Because we had so many other things to be grateful for. As I stood in the banqueting hall of our castle, wearing flowers in my hair and a blue silk gown, I caught Alejandro's eyes across the crowd. And I suddenly didn't see all the princes and farmers, starlets and secretaries, or the happy mix of our neighbors and friends. I didn't see the champagne, or the amazing food, or the flowers hung joyously across the rafters amid a profusion of music and laughter. When I met my husband's gaze, I shivered, and no one else existed.

Alejandro had contacted a lawyer and confessed everything. With the lawyer's advice, he'd thrown himself on the mercy of the court. As Maurine's DNA test had proved, he was the duke's heir, and his only heir at that, and so the group of nobles who oversaw this type of thing decided to allow him to keep his title. He'd also kept the name. Apparently the combination of money and being a direct blood descendant made a big difference. Suddenly, no one was using the word *fraud*.

The scandal was intense, though. For weeks, our castle had been under siege, with crowds of reporters shaking our gates, clamoring for a picture or an interview. But since no one on the estate or in the nearby town would talk, even the scandal died eventually, especially when the Hollywood star I'd seen at Alejandro's party in Madrid had been discovered naked, drunk and belligerent at the base of the Eiffel Tower. Bless her heart. The paparazzi eventually melted away, as our story was old news. Just in time for our reception today, too.

Tomorrow was Alejandro's birthday. His *real* birthday. I would give him the painting of Miguel and Maurine, and show him the brand-new photo album I'd begun for our family. On the back page, I'd tucked in a picture of a sonogram. We were going to have another baby sometime next summer, when the jacaranda trees were in bloom.

I could hardly wait to give Alejandro his gift....

I heard a clank of silverware against crystal. "Everyone. Could I have your attention?" Looking up, I saw Alejandro holding up his champagne glass. "I'd like to thank all our family and friends for coming today...."

"Any time you want to send your private jet," someone shouted.

"Or first-class tickets!"

"Or help me pave my garden path—how's Wednesday?"

There was scattered laughter, and a few tipsy cheers.

Alejandro grinned. "I'd also like to thank my grandmother for doing such a wonderful job designing this party...."

"Darn straight," Maurine said stoutly, holding our smiling baby in her arms. Miguel, though barefoot as he did not like shoes, was suitably dressed in a baby tuxedo.

"I'd like to thank our baby son for sleeping so well at night…."

Darn straight, I echoed, but didn't say aloud.

"But most of all—" Alejandro's dark eyes glowed with tenderness that took my breath away as he looked at me "—I'd like to thank my beautiful wife. Lena. You gave me the family I never dreamed I could have. Just waking up in your arms every morning is a heaven beyond what any mortal man should deserve. But I will spend the rest of my life trying." He held up the flute. "To family. Forever."

"Family forever," everyone cried, with the greatest cheer of all.

"Thank you," I said to them. I blinked fast, smiling with tears in my eyes. "I love you all." I looked at my husband. "Especially you."

Coming through the crowd, Alejandro took me in his arms, and kissed me soundly in front of everyone. And I kissed him back. Oh, boy, you bet I did.

It was crazy. Just a year ago, I'd been so scared and alone. I'd hated Alejandro. I'd thought I would remain a single mother forever.

The disastrous night we were married in Madrid, Alejandro said sometimes fate chooses better for us than we can choose for ourselves. But I think there's more to it.

It's not just fate. You create your own future, step by step, by being brave. By doing the right thing. By telling the truth. By trying your best.

By reaching for the man you love, and giving him the chance to reach back, pull you into his arms and finally show you the man he really is inside—the powerful, infuriating, sexy, compassionate man whom no one else will ever truly know.

Love, like trust, is earned. It is kept, day by day, night by night, as we reveal to each other who we were. Who we are. And most of all, who we hope to be.

* * * * *